Dawg Tales

S.W. Smith

SOLMAR
PUBLISHING
COMPANY, LLC

Solmar Publishing Company, LLC
129 Church Street, Suite 420
New Haven, CT 06510
(203) 772-1344
(888) GLORY-90
www.solmarpublishing.com

The author can be contacted at:
swilk10@cs.com

Editors:Margaret A.Wilkerson, Robert A. Moore
Graphic Design: Christopher Miller, Brian Thompson

Solmar Publishing Company, LLC
129 Church Street, Suite 420
New Haven, CT 06510
(203) 772-1344
(888) GLORY-90
www.solmarpublishing.com

The author can be contacted at:
swilk10@cs.com

TO ALL WHO WANT IT ALL.

Dawg Tales

CHAPTER ONE

SHEENA

Playing by the rules never got me anywhere. That's why I started making my own rules. Even the day I was born, my first day of life, I got fucked over by my own mother. She had the nerve to name me Sheman. Mom got knocked up with me when she was seventeen and tried to get my father to marry her, but he refused. Come to find out, he preferred men to women and was just drunk the night he fucked her. She knew he was gay all along, but she had a bet with her girlfriends that her pussy was so good she could convert and pussy whup any man. She lost the bet because my father, until the day he

1

died preferred dicks to pussies. My father's name was Sherman. To piss him off, she named me She- Man. I call myself Sheena.

Mom ran the streets and wasn't ever home. She didn't care if she had a child. That was not going to stop her fun. Mom started using drugs after I was born. The delivery at Charity Hospital was rough for her. The only way the doctors could get me out was by a C-section. The doctor on duty at the time was an intern and he butchered her. She always blamed me for her drug use. Her excuse was the coke could stop the pain. She tried coke first, and by the time I was five she was head-over-heels addicted to heroin.

She hired cable TV to baby-sit me and didn't give a fuck what I watched. When I was ten, my favorite movies were Scarface, Boyz In The Hood, Goodfellas, The Godfather, and old Dirty Harry movies. The more violent the flick, the more I enjoyed it. I didn't even mind living in the Magnolia Projects. I got to witness cold-blooded murder at least three times a week. I was comforted by that stuff; it was my fix. Normal people needed good music or a line of coke to survive. I had to have murder. Chances are you saw me on the news: the skinny, barefoot child behind the yellow tape at the scene of a shooting. I would have been beaming, thrilled to see the blood leave those lifeless bodies. Even seeing the guts and mushed up brains turned me on. Death certainly never scared me. I imagined myself killing people the way other children fantasized about being firemen.

Growing up, my father was good to me. He paid for my tuition at Holy Ghost Catholic School and made sure that I had clean clothes to wear and plenty of food to eat. He knew I was home alone alot and would come by at times to keep me company. Mom never let him have visitation at his own house, and he figured because of his lifestyle it would be a losing battle taking her to court. So he'd just show up at the apartment when Mom was out partying and made sure I had everything I needed.

The other kids would always tease me about him. They would run around me, screaming, "fag," "sweetie" and "cock-sucker." I pretended I could handle it, but inside I would boil. I'd think of all the ways I could hurt those little bastards and make them pay. In the fifth grade I devised a plan to rid myself of one of the worst offenders.

Kareem was a big head, brown-haired boy who'd been kept back about 35 times. Since he was older than the rest of the class, he was the biggest and bullied everybody, well, everybody but me. Kareem tried to tease me from the moment I got to school until the time I left. He was considered one of the popular boys in school because of his size and his torment of me. The other children laughed when he made jokes about my father's lifestyle. His abuse got more intense everyday. I knew I could not let this situation continue. People got killed over less every single day. I knew I could get rid of that fool, and it thrilled me. I had seen it done in the movies and on the streets. When someone disrespected you, you got rid of whoever it was, no matter what. Even as a fifth grader, I knew that was just the way the world operated.

I began to take note of Kareem's actions after school. I would follow him without his knowing it. He was pretty routine. At 3:15, when the bell rang, he played in the schoolyard for about an hour before he began his journey home, a three-block walk from the school. He didn't live in the projects and had to pass a number of abandoned buildings on the way home. There were only boarded up houses on one of the blocks he had to pass, and it was there that I decided to make my move. Every day after school for two weeks, I hid in one of the buildings with a three- inch thick metal pipe. Because Kareem left school so late, he usually walked home alone. The day I bashed his head in, there was no one else on that block but him and me. I waited until he had passed the building where I was hiding. I jumped out of the door and smacked his back hard with the pipe. He turned toward me and fell simultaneously. I just smiled at him when his head hit the ground. "Who's the fag now, punk?" I laughed. The second whack to his head split it open like a watermelon and his blood gushed onto my socks. I dropped the pipe and ran home, knowing this would not be my last time.

It was shortly after that I started hanging with Coal, Tamara, Kelli, and Rodney at school. They were also the brunt of Kareem's taunts—Coal because he was a dark chocolate complexion, Tamara because she had big breasts, Kelli because she was the smartest in the class, and Rodney because he was quiet. The day after I killed Kareem, I went to school and told each one of them that they didn't have to worry about being teased anymore. They were relieved and didn't even blink an eye when the teacher announced something bad had happened to Kareem and he wouldn't be returning to school. We became fast and inseparable friends after that time. They were like my family, brothers and sisters I never had. They started coming to my home and keeping me company every day after school.

By the time I was fifteen, my mom died of AIDS. And no, she didn't get it from my dad, but from one of those dirty needles she was always using. She was diagnosed with it four years before she passed and had started receiving Social Security benefits to supplement her welfare checks. My dad paid for her funeral expenses, and with her checks still coming in, I was able to survive. The rent in the project was cheap, so I decided to stay there. I was now the woman of the house and I started buying guns with any spare money I could find. I first brought a .44 Magnum. Hell, I had seen Clint Eastwood blow a lot of mutherfuckas away with it, so I figured I could do the same. I then followed with a Beretta, an AK-47, UZI, Tec-9 and then a Glock—everything a growing girl needs. At some point I had enough arsenal to light up a bank. I had silencers and even made some of my own for guns that silencers were not made for. I started taking Karate lessons from the community center, and when I became too advanced for that group, I started Tae Kwon Do with a local master. I had an after school job by then flipping burgers at the local hamburger joint. Between that and my mom's check I had enough change to indulge in my childhood dream of becoming a killing machine, an assassin for hire. Now I make all my money by killing, and it sure beats the hell out of flipping burgers. I only use the best equipment including a Korth Combat .22 caliber and a Para 12.45 pistol for concealed carrying.

But whenever I saw my father, I'd get sick. He wore women's clothes and shook his tail around the projects like he owned the place. I felt love and hate toward my father. I knew he was there when my mom wasn't, but his lifestyle had always made me sick. I kept the pain to myself; I wanted to use it to make myself stronger and tougher. I didn't even shed a tear the day I found out he had died. He had gotten into a catfight with his lover. When the police found his body he had ten stab wounds in the chest.

I primarily did hits for Coal, but I had other clients too. When a mutherfucka messed up, I got the call. It was not like regular life when you didn't pay your bills and ignored the collection calls or answered the phone and pretended you were not home. In my world when you didn't pay your fucking bills, I got the call, and you were dead.

I started out doing hits for Coal's brother, Marcus, but Coal used my services a lot more than his brother ever did. He knew there was a lot of competition out there and a lot of mutherfuckas would try to snatch your shit in a minute and eliminate you and your money. Since Bush got elected, money was tight and people would do anything to get it and keep it. Sometimes Coal would pay me more to kill someone than the actual amount owed just to keep respect and to run a tight ship. I liked my job so I didn't care what his reasons were. Just give me the right amount of cash and I would get the job done. To hell with a 9 to 5, the stuff I did was the bomb.

My last victim met me at the Brown Derby for a

drink. I'd been following him to this bar for the last three nights. I approached him like I was a hooker. I could do things like that because I looked like a model when I wanted to. I had that long brown hair and a smooth dark brown complexion with small lips and a sharp nose. I knew how to dress, having picked up my sense of fashion from my father. I even took some of his clothes when he died. And being 5'8" with long shapely legs to complement, I could wear the hell out of a skirt.

That night I saw my target at the bar, approached him and told him I would do anything he wanted me to for $50. He readily agreed since I quoted him such a good price. He got a hotel room, and once inside, I gave him the fuck of his life. I had him sit on the edge of the bed, then I pulled down his pants and started stroking his dick gently with soft smooth strokes of my tongue. After some time I increased my speed, letting my teeth gently tease the shaft of his penis. Knowing that a lot of men's breasts are more sensitive than women's, I grabbed the nipples on his chest and squeezed them hard as I sucked him. His hands held my head steady on him, but I managed to push his back flat on the bed. I sucked on him so long and hard he exploded in my mouth and I greedily swallowed his juices. I was so horny after that that when he wanted to put it in my ass, I happily agreed. I made him put on a rubber cause I decided a long time ago I wasn't going out like my mama. It felt good as he eased his long dick inside me. Hell, it felt good when he got rough and pushed my face on the bed and began ramming it into me.

When I came, I came hard. He came again right after me and was so tired he lay flat on his back, closed his eyes, and just grinned. As I put on my clothes, I told him how good he was and how I had never been fucked like that before. I promised that if he met me at the same hotel tomorrow, I would give him some more for free, he was so good. He started laughing and said, "Yeah, I been told that before." His eyes and mouth widened as he glimpsed my 45 Silencer. I shot him straight in the forehead. It was a shame, a waste of good meat, but a girl gotta do what a girl gotta do. I grabbed a washcloth and wiped his dick clean before I pushed him off the bed. I tossed the sheets and bedspread into a plastic bag I had in my purse. No sense leaving DNA for the police. Out the back door of the hotel I ran into the muggy night, happy for the groove and satisfied at another job well done.

S.W. Smith

CHAPTER TWO

KELLI

The only way I paid for law school was to keep everybody high. I sold drugs to the students and to the professors and administrators on campus. I sold everything that you could have ever imagined. Chronic, crack, cocaine, whatever, whenever.

If it weren't for my hustling ass father, I probably wouldn't have even gone to law school. I was the oldest of seven children he had with my mother. Total, he might have had about twenty children with about seven different women. He and Moms were legally married, but she was the only one respecting the vows. She knew he was

11

a whore, but it never seemed to bother her. He would only spend about three nights a week at home. The man never had a real job, and when he would actually get some employment, it usually only lasted about six months. It was funny though—his ass was never broke.

He said he was meant to be a hustler, and his job was the streets. Every day on the way home from Holy Ghost school, I would see him hanging on the corner of Freret and LaSalle Street across from the Magnolia housing project holding court with his friends. He had the gift of gab. My father was the smoothest talker, I mean, he could probably sell ice cream to Eskimos. That is probably how he convinced so many women to have his babies. He wasn't a good-looking man, short about 5'6", bald, and semi-muscular. He always kept himself clean, though, and smelling good with fancy cologne and freshly ironed clothes. Sometimes he would be playing dice, other times cards, but most of the time he stuck to selling dope. He would stop me and start his preaching about how smart I was and how he really needed one of his children to be a lawyer to keep him and his friends out of jail. He would say, "There is a hard way to make money and an easy way to make money. Get a law degree, and you always have the easy way. Make sure you stay your ass in school."

Dad would even take the time from his activities

to check my homework and go over my grades. He would sit me down on the stoop next to his street corner and rifle through my school bag. After this was done he would hand me $20 and tell me to go on about my business. He would always let me know, though, the minute my grades slipped, that I wasn't getting shit from him. Since mom worked a regular 9 to 5 as a nurse's aide, her money was always short and stretched between seven children; I never saw any of it. So to keep the funds flowing from my father, I had to produce good test scores. This went on until I finished Fortier High school when he was killed trying to rob a bank in New Orleans East. I had already been accepted into Loyola University in New Orleans and school was to start in two weeks. I believe to this day he robbed that bank to try to get my tuition money. I had gotten some scholarship and financial aid but not enough to cover the full tuition and room and board, so I had told him I was going to take off a year and save some money. The last conversation I had with him was on that same street corner where he checked my grades every day.

"Ain't no way I am going to be able to go to college living at home. Too many distractions, too much noise with all them children running around. I didn't get enough money to stay on campus, so I will just chill awhile, make some quick doe and go back later."

"It is my experience that people who quit never go back. Look, I wanted to be a lawyer too. I had the same idea: quit school, make cash, and then go back. But I got caught up in the streets: babies to feed, women to keep and twenty years later I am still out here hustling. Every time I see that bad mutherfucka Johnny Cochran on TV, I know I could have been in his shoes right now if I hadn't quit. Don't you quit. I will find the money for you but you gotta stay your ass in school, and don't come out until you are a lawyer."

"I don't know, I will get back to you on that," were the last words I spoke to him before I hurried home. On the ten o'clock news, I learned he was shot dead coming out of the bank.

My mom had a wake for him one week later at Labat's Funeral home on Washington Avenue about two miles from our home. All his other children showed up as well as his other women. Although my mom paid for the burial policy that covered his funeral expenses, those other bitches came in there like they were running the show. They tried to tell the funeral director how the funeral should be handled. They even bombarded my mom with questions about what money my father left and how they were going to feed their kids since he was gone. She didn't answer any of them. Mom just walked in front of the opened casket.

"Hell no," she shouted. "We ain't having this shit here. I am the only mutherfucka paying for this shit and I am the only mutherfucka dictating how Clyde is going to be buried. Anybody who don't like that shit, need to start stepping, or I will kick their ass right here, right now."

I was in shock, I never heard Mom talk like that. She was so busy working most of the time and caring for my younger sister and brothers, I never spent any real time with her or made a connection with her. In other words, I never really knew her. I don't think she loved my father all that much, but she had been disrespected for so long I guess she figured for the last time in his presence she would have some respect.

Unfortunately, the other women weren't seeing it that way, and three of them stormed the casket and started swinging at my mother. One of them grabbed her hair and the other two started throwing body punches. The force they propelled caused my mom to fall on the casket, pushing it off its stand. My dad's body.fell to the floor. I jumped up and said, "Fuck this shit," and grabbed two of those bitches off my mother. They were no match for me. I body slammed both of them together like two flapjacks, and they fell hard to the ground. They both hit the floor and I just started stomping and kicking each of them with my brand new Staci Adams heels. I kicked one a few times and then started kicking the other. I probably would have killed both of those bitches but for the fact my friend Rodney pulled me away and out of the funeral home. The cops pulled up as we were leaving. Mom was kicking ass too and damn near killed her attacker. Unfortunately, the police pulled her off the woman and dragged her out of the funeral home with half of her weave pulled from her head. I saw her being shoved in the police car. They kept her in jail a week and she missed the burial.

The next day I buried my father at Lakelawn cemetery in the presence of my six siblings. At his gravesite, I made the promise that I would finish law school so that his death would not be in vain.

CHAPTER THREE

COAL

Coal always knew his mother Juanita liked his brother Marcus better than him. Marcus was only five-years older than Coal, but they had different daddies. Where Coal's skin was the color of charcoal, Marcus's skin was fair brown. Coal's hair was tight and nappy, and Marcus's hair was wavy and easy to comb.

Juanita used to always tell Coal when he was growing up that Marcus was a better baby than he was. She always compared the two, especially when she was drunk, which was most of the time. According to Juanita, Marcus always made her happy, and Coal made her cry

17

from day one. For the first fifteen years of his life, Coal was told that Marcus was bigger, smarter, and more handsome than he was. That Marcus would grow up to make his mother proud and Coal wouldn't grow up to be shit. Funny thing though is, Coal believed every word of it growing up. He worshipped the ground Marcus walked on and he always felt inferior to him.

When Marcus did something wrong, Coal usually got the blame. His mother would beat him so hard that he thought she was really trying to "beat the black off of him," as his mother would so often say.

Marcus would always let Coal hang around him. He would order Coal around all the time. Coal didn't mind, he just wanted to be around Marcus who did treat him better than his mother.

The rest of the time Coal would spend with Kelli, Sheena, and Rodney. He always bossed them around and they would follow his orders. That was how he got the first taste of power. He would direct them to do evil things too. Coal would have them beat up other schoolmates, steal lunch money, cut class, and change grades in teachers' record book.

Around the time of high school, Rodney started acting differently toward Coal. He would no longer follow Coal's orders. They were still friends in high school, but Rodney would spend more time studying and less time hanging with Coal. Coal was hurt that Rodney would not spend as much time with him, but he didn't bother him about it.

Gradually, Marcus began hustling and so did Coal. Marcus formed a group called the Cash Dawgs which consisted of his buddies from the street. Coal followed suit and called his gang,-Kelli, Sheena, and Rodney-Money Dawgs.

Marcus's gang terrorized the streets. They took over the Magnolia Project with a vengeance. They primarily dealt coke. The only thing that stood between them and total glory over the streets were the Jungle Brothers. Coal wanted so bad to work with Marcus that Marcus had him work the streets, first as a lookout, then actually in sales. Coal wanted to move up to management, and run his own crew, but Marcus never allowed this to happen. Both boys continued to live at home with their mother who was pleased that Marcus was bringing in a lot of extra money to fix up the apartment they lived in and to buy groceries and clothes. Marcus would spend lavishly on his mother. He brought her jewelry, watches, and designer clothing. No matter what Coal brought her, Juanita was never satisfied. He tried hard to please his mother. He wanted to make her love him like she loved Marcus. Even if he tried to hug her, she would always say to him, "Get off me, boy." It would hurt Coal when

Juanita told him that, but he would just try to laugh it off.

Finally Marcus had enough money to move the family out of the Magnolia Project to New Orleans East in the suburbs. Coal was not thrilled about it. He decided that since he never really got any love from his brother and mother, his real people were in the Magnolia. So there, he would stay.

Marcus and Coal fell out over the fact that Coal decided to stay in the old apartment.

"Lookie here, bro, I think it's time for us to make a move outta here. It's getting too hot down here and I think we can have a good life in the east."

"Man, my peeps are down here. I can't abandon them. Size, I'm thinking about setting up my own shop."

"What do you mean, set up your own shop?" Marcus was afraid of the competition.

"I don't take care of you enough, you ingrate mutherfucka?"

"Naw man, its not that; it's just I am tired of being called little Marcus. It's time for me to be my own man."

"Own man! Man, you ain't never gonna do shit." Once Marcus said that he wished he could take it back. He knew that his relationship with Coal would never be the same after that. Something he would always regret.

Coal was hurt that Marcus had believed the same thing their mamma believed. Right then and there he knew that Marcus never had his back and he would no longer have his.

"Whatever, man, whatever."

Coal walked away to set up his own shop.

S.W. SMITH

CHAPTER FOUR

KELLI

I started school the following week and knew quickly I had to make up for half of the money I didn't have to stay there. I got a dormitory room and immediately set up shop. I promised myself I would not get greedy: just make enough to finish paying off the tuition. Since most of the students in the dormitories were from out of state upper middle class homes, I knew I had a ready market for any drug I chose to sell. I just had to get my supply together. I contacted my friend Coal whose brother, Marcus, was in the business and asked him to hook me up. He was reluctant, but I explained to him that there were no other funds available for me to stay in school and that my intent was to quit as soon as I made enough money to get through law school. Coal was always like a big brother to me throughout grammar school and high school. He and Sheena always made sure no one disrespected me because my grades were good and I was smart. For some reason in the schools I went to in New Orleans none of the students looked up to me because I was smart. I used to be teased constantly and treated like I was some kind of nerd even though I always had on the latest fashion courtesy of my father's money. I hope African Americans start to appreciate one day that intelligence is something that we should encourage among each other.

Since Coal knew me well, getting the drugs from his brother on consignment wouldn't be a problem. The only thing I had to do was make sure that the only people I dealt with would not turn me in. That's where Sheena came in.

I knew Sheena was doing hits. Although she couldn't protect me like she used to, maybe her work could. I called and asked her to come over to the dorm so we could talk. I explained my predicament and asked if she could take pictures of the bodies for me on my digital camera. She loved the idea. I had known for a while what Sheena did for a living, but I never criticized her for it. I actually thought it was kind of cool that she actually made a good living doing what I saw actors do in the movies. Though I had to admit, sometimes I suspected she was too obsessed with death and "two eggs short of a dozen," in other words, a little crazy. Sheena took my camera and brought it back the next week. I downloaded the contents on my computer, and the images I saw were so graphic I almost lost the content of my stomach. She had cut up this man in at least twenty pieces. The crazy thing about the man though was that he was naked and his midsection, that was cut from the rest of his body, still had his torso attached and his penis was standing straight up. I am sure the expression on my face must have given away the horror I felt, but Sheena just laugh at me.

After I showed that to some of the slow payers on campus, revenues from collections really picked up. I finished school in three years and was in the top of my class. I even managed to pledge a sorority while I was in school. My sisters liked to get high and party as much as I did.

Law school was another story though. It was tough and I had to study my butt off. What interested me the most though was criminal law. I made all my best grades in that subject. Analyzing the cases was easy for me because, where I was from, I lived the shit. I participated in moot court and won awards for my arguments.

My side business was going really well, so I didn't have to worry about the tuition. Some of my professors were in to smoking blunt too, so when the classes got too tough I just became their supplier. All of a sudden, my grades improved two-fold.

When that didn't work, I always had my fine body to work with. I didn't look like the typical law student the professors were used to being around. I wore a size 38 C and had a coke-shape body that would put Vivica Fox to shame. To top it off, and I ain't bragging, my butt had been called superior to even JLo's. I also had this gold cap with a diamond put in the side of my mouth that enhanced my wicked smile twofold. I'd seen a lot of hoes with the tooth in the front, which to me is just plain ghetto. Mine was positioned on the side and looked classy.

I must admit I didn't know much about sex and controlling men since I had spent most of my time in the books. I had a few boyfriends in college. Despite my good looks, I suspect I wasn't takin care of the business properly, though, because none of the relationships lasted long. I was never available for late night booty calls, and I never felt like I knew how to give head properly. They offered to teach me, but I never got anything for the lesson, so I figured I wouldn't waste my time. I figured, that later, like anything else, it could be studied and learned.

This one professor who taught a Federal Income

Tax class was flunking me, and I knew in order to graduate I had to take care of him good. I had heard from the grapevine he didn't do drugs. One thing I learned early was that most men only cared about three things: money, sex, or gettin' high. I wasn't about to pay him, so I figured I'd have to fuck to get my point across. He was a balding, somewhat good looking white man in his fifties a cross between Harrison Ford and Mel Gibson. He was probably getting some on a regular basis, but like all white men I knew he secretly desired dark meat.

My first stop was the bookstore. I didn't want any manuals, just something I could enjoy while learning. My classmates were always talking about Zane books, Nubia's book, *More Bounce* and a book called *Caught Up* that were so hot and steamy you could have orgasms while reading them. Shit, there was this one book *Sexaballer* that even showed pictures. I decided to give them a try. My second stop was the video store. I picked up some tapes and it was on. I observed women and men getting sucked and fucked everywhere. This shit turned me on immediately, and I had to put it to action right away. Shit, the tax course was boring; this shit I was learning could really help me.

I saw him the next day and approached him after class when the other students had left. I was dressed in a red low cut outfit that pushed my braless boobs up and

27

gave them a round melon shape. I asked him if I could speak to him privately in his office that afternoon about the last exam he gave.

He readily agreed and I sashayed my butt out in the sexiest manner I could muster. I could feel his eyes following my butt. I knew he would take the bait, and all I had to do was to execute the plan.

At the designated time I appeared at Professor Hogan's office. The office was small and modest with a singular desk and chair on the side. The desk was swamped with books and corrected papers. This time I had on a see through net blouse with a black silky bra underneath. I had changed into the sexiest pair of Calvin Klein shorts I owned, which was about two sizes two small. The edge of the shorts revealed my butt cheeks. I had on my petunia perfume bought from the French Quarter. The lady who sold it said it was a guaranteed aphrodisiac which could drive any man wild. With the exam in my hand, I went over to the side of Mr. Hogan's desk where he sat and showed him the big red F that was marked on the exam. I made sure my breasts were at the level of his eyes as I leaned in next to him.

"Well, Ms West, looking at your test score, I really didn't think you fully comprehended the case material that was assigned. Look at this analysis of United States vs Fulton. You really missed the point here."

"Let me see the case book." I leaned closer to him to grab the book and opened the page to the case. My boobs were darn near under his nose. I saw him sit up a little straighter.

In my sexiest voice I said, "I think Fulton was manipulating the tax from day one. He knew what he wanted from the government and decided to do anything that he could to get what he wanted. So what if he screwed up the company payroll records doing it? The important thing is the satisfaction of the tax bill by the company." I emphasized the words, "manipulate", "get what he wanted" and "screwed". I even began to touch his hands ever so lightly. He picked up on my cues and put his nose into my blouse. He stuck his tongue deep down into the cleavage. I grabbed his penis and held his equipment firmly against his balls. He was packing and I was definitely enjoying the ideas of mixing business with pleasure. His free hand quickly cleared the items on top of the desk to the floor and backed my butt on top of it. His lips hit my mouth as he shoved his long tongue deep inside me.

I felt like I was getting too personal kissing. Plus, his breath, which smelled of red beans and rice, was turning me off, so I eased my mouth down to where my hand held his pants. I zipped down his zipper and his penis exploded onto my face. To my amazement he wasn't wearing any underwear. His penis became limp, but I knew I wasn't going out like that. I wanted to put the techniques I had learned from the DVDs and books to good use. Also I knew I always wanted to fuck Harrison Ford since I saw that movie What Lies Beneath, and was turned on by the hair on Ford's chest, so I figured this would be the closest thing to it.

I sucked his penis like a tender cooked neck bone. I hadn't had any lunch so I hungrily pretended this was my next meal. I must admit I was getting horny by the minute as I proceeded to try to get him hard again. Unfortunately, he smelled of urine and the sperm he had prematurely ejaculated, but I got over it and continued to suck him up like a bowl of file' gumbo.

After about forty-five minutes of serious sucking, nothing would work to bring that limp thing up. My lips were numb, and my knees were cramped. I couldn't continue any longer. I looked up to see Hogan's smiling face.

"I admire your perseverance and endurance. I would imagine you put that type of dedication into your last tax test. Maybe it was short-sighted of me to have flunked you. I think I can change that grade to perhaps a B minus."

In the sexiest Southern accent I could muster, I replied; "Well Professor, two disturbing things happen here today: one, we engaged in oral sex, and two, your equipment malfunctioned. The problem is I can't figure out which would be more damaging to your job and reputation. Of course, with the proper compensation, I will make sure neither comes to light."

"And what exactly will I be taxed for my indiscretion here?"

"Final grade of an A and $500.00."

His smile shifted to a frown as he pulled out a checkbook and wrote a check payable to cash. He opened his grade book to my name, and a line was added to the "F" to make it look like an "A."

"Thank you, professor. If you need any additional tax lessons, just give me a call."

As I walked out of his office I knew right then and there I had the makings of a great lawyer.

CHAPTER FIVE

COAL

Coal felt that the best thing that ever happened to him was when he set up his own shop. He got himself a supplier, but instead of selling coke like Marcus, he sold marijuana. Coal didn't sell the volume that Marcus did, but he figured it was a cleaner business and he had to deal with less violence than Marcus. Where Marcus sold mostly to the neighbors, Coal sold outside the neighborhood to the college crowd and to the middle class who wanted to get high. He thought it was safer and healthier smoking bud than sniffing coke or using crack.

Through the years, he stayed close to Sheena and

Kelli, but lost contact with Rodney when Coal dropped out of high school. When Sheena needed some extra money, he turned her on to Marcus who used her services regularly to get rid of his enemies. When Kelli needed more than marijuana for her clientele, he turned her on to Marcus as well who supplied her with the type of product some of her customers wanted. Marcus and Kelli had gotten tight, they got married and had a baby.

Because Marcus was getting more powerful, the rival group Jungle Boyz wanted to take him down. The violence between the Cash Dawgs and Jungle Boyz had gotten so intense that the city policeman were investigating a murder a day. A task force was formed and the police chief gave the command that the leaders of both groups must be taken down by any means necessary.

Surveillance was started immediately on Marcus by the cops. On top of that, the big money that Marcus was making caused him to be sloppy and he was not as careful about his operations as he was in the past.

Marcus was lazy and at times he would bring the product and money to an apartment he kept as his safe house. At times when he didn't feel like making the drive home, he would stay at the apartment with the drugs and money. When Marcus first started in the business he knew this was a no no because he didn't ever want to be busted with evidence. As his wealth grew, so did his comfort level and he thought he would be King of the Magnolia forever.

Marcus didn't know that the cops had started surveillance on him and that they followed him to the apartment on the days he would bring the product and money there. When they finally did bust him at the apartment, he had 4 kilos of cocaine and $200,000.00 in cash.

Marcus also had the problem of having a jacket and because of his record, he knew he would be facing a long time. The cops had him cold the night they arrested him with drugs and money in his possession.

Because of the quantity of drugs involved, Marcus was held without bond. Marcus felt like a caged animal. He loved the good life too much, and he would do anything to get out.

Coal came to see him two weeks after his arrest. Marcus sounded scared.

"Man, I need you to take this rap for me."

"What are you talking about? I came to see you and you don't say 'Hi' or 'How you doing.' You just ask me to take a bid for you."

"Look man, you don't have any record. First offense, and you will get slapped on the wrist, the lowest they're offering me is fifteen years."

"Marcus, that is the dumbest shit I ever heard, you want me to tell the cops that was my shit even though you were sleeping with it. Be a man and take the time."

"Fuck that, Coal, if I give them some incentives, they would give me a free ride."

"Man, what incentives?"

"You know suppliers, other people running in the game."

Coal was stunned by what he was hearing. He knew his brother was talking about him along with his contacts. It was the second time his brother had pierced his heart.

"Man, I am gonna leave and ignore you ever said that shit cause if you thought about it, I know you wouldn't bring down your own blood."

Coal left the jail with a heavy heart. His cell phone rang.

"Coal, this is your mother. Did you see Marcus today?"

"I saw him. What's up?"

She cried. "I think you need to do this thing Marcus asked of you. You know he can't do the time like you could. I need him here with me, I can't lose my son to that zoo."

Coal was hurt by her request. "Oh, but you can lose your other son cause you don't give a shit about him. Remember, I am not going to be shit anyway. Ma, I have no intention of ever having a conversation with you again.

Don't ever call me again." He hung up.

Coal knew what he had to do now. He went to Marcus' suppliers and told them of Marcus' plan. They were so grateful, they offered to set Coal up to take over Marcus' territory. Coal agreed and was on his way to setting up his own empire. He ruled with a more iron fist than Marcus and he promised himself he wouldn't get caught like his brother. Eventually, he did put out more product and made more money than Marcus ever did.

Two weeks later, Marcus was dead.

S.W. Smith

CHAPTER SIX

SHEENA

I told Coal that shit wasn't going to work from day one. He had me put some poison in some motherfucka's drink because he saw some gangsta kill someone that way in a movie. He didn't want anyone to know Larry was murdered because he was Coal's cousin, so he figured the best way was to poison him and let everyone think he died of natural causes. Coal was tired of him playing on his name. Coal had to provide protection for him because he was related, but Cuz figured he didn't have to pay Coal since they were related. More importantly, he was messing with other relationships Coal had.

Even though I knew it was only the beginning of trouble, that killing this way was dumb shit, I still got the tasteless poison from this Haitian voodoo queen I knew in the French Quarter. She said it would take a few days, but it was effective. I knew this mug was a dancer and every Friday night he would be on the dance floor showing off his steps at Pampies, a nightclub on St Bernard Avenue. The night I got rid of him, this dude had on a striped leopard fur coat and had pressed his hair until it was down his back. He looked like a young Snoop Dog. I eyed him sipping a drink with two young chicken heads that seem to be fascinated with every word that he said. The club was packed. The music was jamming that night. The DJ was playing all the right numbers, Right Thur, by Chingy and Shake a Tail Feather by Nelly, P Diddy and Murphy. The mug wouldn't move from his table until P.I.M.P. by 50 Cents started blasting from the speakers. He jumped up and started moving toward the dance floor with one girl in each arm.

I slid over to his table bopping my head and arm to the beat of the music and poured the poison in his cup. The dude was drinking an apple martini. What a weak ass drink, I thought, as I walked away from the table. He returned to his table with the two girls after the song ended. He took a small sip from his glass. One of the girls must have said something to him, because he backhand slapped her so hard she hit the floor before I had a chance to get back to my position. He got up, took one girl by the arm, grabbed the other girl by her hair and dragged them both out of the club.

Shit, I have to get the rest of that fucking drink I thought, as I boogied back to the table. I grabbed it just as the waitress was pulling the glasses off the table. Now I'd have to wait to see if the stuff really worked.

I had to trail this mutherfucka for five days. It was sickening. He really thought he was a real pimp. He had those two chicken heads working for him. Any time a real pimp would complain that his girls were infringing on their territory, he would draw Coal's name like a revolver, and the other pimp would naturally back down. I could see why Coal wanted to kill his cousin, especially since the other pimps were paying Coal a piece of their action. Anyway, the mutherfucka still seem healthy to me. I started to call that voodoo bitch back one night when I was sitting outside his apartment, but I saw the flashing lights of an ambulance pull up ten feet in front of my car. The attendants ran in and brought Larry out on a stretcher. He was brought to Charity Hospital where he lapsed into a coma.

Three days later when I told Coal what happened, he exploded. "The mutherfucka is in a coma and still alive. What the hell do I pay you for?"

I didn't say a word. I headed straight to the hospital and got a pass to see Larry and went up to his room to finish the job. When I got there he was by himself, his body attached to at least ten tubes. I grabbed one of the pillows from under his head to suffocate him when I saw the shadow of a man enter the room. With the pillow still in my hand, I turned around to see one of the most gorgeous men I had ever laid eyes on, Doctor Clarence Woods, an ebony colored brother with curly hair and big brown eyes.

"I was trying to make him more comfortable. Do you think my cousin is going to make it?" I said with the most tearful eyes I could muster.

"I don't know; we have no idea why his body shut down. We are still doing tests, but things don't look good. I am Clarence Woods." He reached out his hand to touch mine.

My panties were getting damp with just the touch of his hand. "I know I saw your tag, Doctor, I really appreciate what you are doing for Larry."

"I am trying my hardest, but I am really sorry I can't do more."

"Are you from New Orleans? You sound like you are from up north somewhere."

I wanted to get to know more about Dr. Woods.

"Actually, I am from Chicago. I am here doing

my residency and I am getting a lot of experience at this hospital. I have been here two years and my term is almost up."

We talked for the next two-hours, and he seemed to be as attracted to me as I was to him. When a page came for him to go see another patient, he said, "Look, I know it is inappropriate to ask you this while your cousin is like this, but could I see you again sometime outside of the hospital?"

"Yes, when do you want to meet?"

"How about tomorrow night? It's my only day off this week. Do you like spicy food? I like a restaurant named Copelin's. It's on St. Charles Avenue."

"I will meet you at eight o'clock."

"I gotta run, I'll check on your cousin again later."

I could not bring myself to kill Larry once Clarence left. I left the hospital with joyful anticipation of what a relationship with a doctor would be like.

CHAPTER SEVEN

KELLI

I don't believe this motherfucka has me waiting for him so long. That bitch is about to get cut from my stable. I am pissed, and this dude is about to feel the wrath of my anger. Who the fuck does he think he is, having me waiting in front of this BMW dealer for twenty minutes? I will fuck him up good. He knows he is suppose to buy me this 745 for my birthday and if I don't get it, that's his ass.

Randolph Jefferson's fat ass finally showed up ten minutes later.

"I have been out here thirty minutes, and I was

about to do something you would have regretted for a very long time, Mr. Jefferson."

"Look baby, I was a little late transferring funds. You know it wouldn't be good for either of us if my wife found out about this."

"I don't give a fuck if your wife finds out about this. If I had to wait any longer, she was going to find out about it from me. You have gotten fucked better than you ever been fucked before in your life. You should have had this shit taken care of a long time ago. Don't think I wasn't serious about cutting you off if I didn't get my car. Now go in there and get the paper work done.'

I began my affair with Randolph about one year ago. Jefferson was the CEO and majority shareholder of Welltown Oil, a company based in New Orleans that did about fifty million dollars of business last year processing crude fuel. He was deathly pale and balding-probably the ugliest white man I ever fucked, but he was one of the wealthiest. I starting fucking him about two weeks after I became his lawyer. Since I charged him double my normal fee, my paycheck had fattened drastically, and the law firm I worked for was thrilled. It had only taken me a week to make my presence known to Jefferson. He had initially retained John Tate, another lawyer in my office. The two usually came into the office late. One night he was sitting in Tate's office. Since I was working late, I offered to bring him coffee. Tate had gone to look for some paper work and I just stepped on in with my short skirt which emphasized my big booty and my skin-tight blouse which I no longer concealed under my coat jacket. I brought in two cups of coffee and handed him one, as I inched my breasts closer to his view. His eyes almost popped out of their sockets when my cleavage came within two inches of his nose. Then I spilled the contents of the other cup onto my blouse.

"I am so clumsy. Look what I just did!" I screamed. I placed the coffee cup on Tate's desk and began opening my blouse and wiping the stain with my hand. I handed him a tissue and asked him if he could help me get the stain off. I had never seen a man's hand shake so hard.

"I offer great legal advice. If you need a real lawyer who can offer your company a variety of services, and who can go beyond the call of duty, just tell John here you want me as lead counsel."

I put my card into his shirt. The next day he called the senior partner and told them he wanted me to be his new lawyer. I figured that he would drop Tate like a hot potato. I had seen him and his wife in the society section of the Times Picayune, and they both looked pretty homey. His hanging belly and droopy eyes convinced me he needed a good fuck and that he would pay dearly for it. I figured right. Since we'd been together, I'd received five tennis bracelets with enough bling bling to lighten up a pitch-black room. His generosity had also contributed to my gold ring collection and the number of Benjamins in my bank account. The crazy thing about it was that he was happy with me giving it to him only once a week. We meet at the Clarion on Canal Street always at 2p.m. on Friday about six blocks from where I go to work. The rest of the time we would work on his company's legal problems.

Well, he'd been promising me this new car for quite some time and not that something was wrong with the 2002 model 745 that I had, I really wanted the 2004 edition with the Presidential package: three screens, DVD player, Direct TV hookup, navigation system, tinted windows, bullet-proof glass, and reinforced steel doors. That alone added three thousand pounds to the car. A girl could never be too careful especially in my line of work. I had planned to hook up the wheels with some 22 inch Astanti Cellina with an 8-inch lip once I got it. I had even picked them out already, and they were just waiting for the car.

I waited outside for him while he was completing the paperwork. He brought out a set of keys with a big grin on his face.

"I special ordered yours just like I promised. The

salesman said it would take at least four weeks to come in, but in the meantime you can drive any one of the floor models in there. Happy, baby?"

"Yeah, I am happy." I rubbed my hand on his equipment as my lips licked his face. "I will show you how happy I am as soon as you let me."

"Well, I'll call you after my afternoon meeting because I need my lawyer real bad."

I blew him a kiss as he backed toward his car. The last thing I wanted to do was to fuck him tonight, but I guess I had to show my appreciation. I wanted to get more goodies, and I'd do whatever it took to get them. Next time he was gonna have to buy me a Maybach, I thought.

I went inside the dealership and saw various BMWs on the show room floor. I immediately selected a red M3 Coupe with a convertible top. I opened the door and placed myself snugly into the seat. I closed my eyes as the car salesman described all the features.

"Would you just back the fuck up? You are messing with my mood. I already bought a car, I am just trying to figure out which one of these bad boys is gonna be my loaner until my quarter to eight arrives."

This feels good. You know you got power when you sitting in one of these. I should have told Randolph to buy this one. I will wait about six months and tap him again.

"Excuse me, Miss. I can do the paperwork for you anytime you like."

"Didn't I just tell you....?" I looked up over the windshield and stared hard. I hadn't seen him in a while, but he looked good. Rodney Roberts. He had gotten fine since the last time I saw him in the eighth grade:curly hair, muscular body, and a bronze tone to his dark yellow complexion.

"Rodney! What's up Dawg?" I jumped out the car and gave him a big hug.

"I haven't seen you since high school. What have you been up to?"

He smiled and his too big dimples appeared.

"I'm doin' all right. I hear you're a big time lawyer now. I always knew you were smart enough to go places."

"You too. So what's your nine to five?"

"I am with International Postal Services."

"Yeah, what exactly do you do for them?"

Rodney seemed ashamed. "I deliver packages."

My excitement at seeing Rodney diminished. "Well it's a job somebody has to do."

"I am looking at some other things."

"Well, here is my card. If you decide to do some other things, let me know. You may need me." I smiled.

His friend Jamal walked up. From the looks of him, I could tell he was in the delivery business as well. Both men were typical IPS drivers: muscular, fine as they wanted to be, but from the looks of their shoes and clothes, broke.

"Rodney! Man! You just walked away and I see why."

"Wait, man, I am talking to my lawyer." Rodney smiled at me and grabbed my hand. "I will call you later." He put my card in his pocket.

I smiled as I watched him and his friend walk away. It was too bad Rodney never did anything with himself. I definitely felt an attraction to him, but he would never be able to take care of me working at IPS.

CHAPTER EIGHT

RODNEY

The alarm clock went off, and Rodney's hand hit it so hard the clock fell. He woke up to a model of tennis shoes dangling from the ceiling. Across the entire room there were drawings of tennis shoes. A symbol of a bullet was displayed on each drawing. He walked over to the mirror, wiped his eyes and picked up a pair of tennis shoes. Rodney wanted desperately to own his own business, a tennis shoe factory.

He looked at himself in the mirror and shouted. "Bullet Tennis Shoes will make you run faster than a bullet and shoot the ball like a pistol." Rodney kissed the tennis shoe. "Me and you baby are going places."

He got dressed in his brown uniform and placed his cap squarely on his head. On top of the cap were the letters IPS. He grabbed his tablet off the table with his delivery schedules and went outside to where his truck was waiting. On the truck were the words, "We Deliver On Time."

CHAPTER NINE

RODNEY

Rodney was bone tired at the end of his shift as he arrived at the IPS warehouse. The most dreaded time of the day for Rodney was when he had to report in with the rest of the drivers to turn in his invoices. As he was waiting in line to turn in his slips, he saw Jamal talking in the corner to a group of fellas. Suddenly there was an outburst of laughter. Rodney knew what it was all about-the reason he hated coming to the warehouse-the dream killers. All those guys wanted to do was be delivery boys all their lives. Because Rodney wanted to do bigger things, he was the butt of all their jokes. Their mission was to kill his dreams.

"I am serious, I just be looking at the beamers, but Rodney thinks he's actually going to buy one, along with this mansion in Eastover. Oh and don't forget the pool and tennis court!!! He already got his crib picked out. It's the one next to Baby's house from Cash Money Records." The crowd erupted into laughter.

Rodney walked up and gave Jamal an evil eye. He started to speak but decided against it and walked away.

"All from a pair of tennis shoes," Jamal uttered under his breath.

Rodney's next stop was the manager's office where he had to endure his monthly evaluation. A chubby white man was sitting behind an oak desk eyeing a stack of papers. He barely acknowledged Rodney's presence.

"Punctual, hardworking, hmmm, good attitude. Well this is a very positive evaluation."

"Thank you."

"We have been watching you very closely for the last few years and we think you should be in a management position. Heck, you have the right qualities."

"I am glad I'm doing a good job, but my goals are not to be a manager, I want to own my own business, a tennis shoe factory. I don't mean to sound unappreciative, but if I took a management position, it would mean more hours and more responsibilities which mean less time for me to handle my own business."

"Rodney, I like you and I have been supervising you for a while. Let me break it down to you-the company is about to do some downsizing and because of your pay level, if you don't move up you are going to be laid off and replaced by a new hire whom they can pay less money. Now the supervisor position I am offering you won't pay much more then you are making now, and yeah, you will have more responsibilities and more hours, but at least you will have a job."

"Damn, that's some fucked up shit."

"Look man, I don't need the profanity in my office, but I understand what you're going through. Take two weeks, think about it and let me know. After that, all bets are off."

"I hear you. I will let you know in two weeks."

CHAPTER TEN

RODNEY

Rodney had about fifteen minutes left on his lunch when he decided to pull the card out of his wallet. Kelli West, Attorney at Law. He pulled his cell phone out of his shirt pocket and dialed the number.

"Ms. West, please."

The reception buzzed Kelli's office. Kelli picked up the receiver.

"Hello, Attorney West."

"Hi. Remember me? I told you I would call."

"Well, I am kind of busy right now, I can't talk......"

"Aw, come on, I barely said hello and you are trying to get off the phone. I remember when you had long pig tails and couldn't stop running your mouth on the school playground."

A smile came to Kelli's face. "Really. I am busy."

"OK, just tell me quickly, will you go out to eat with me?"

"Well, I don't really know if I can find the time...." Rodney cut her off.

"Look, I know right now I deliver packages for a living and you're a lawyer, but we have a lot of history together. Let's catch up on old times and maybe have some fun."

Kelli hesitated and a long silence ensured.

"Oh I see, just because I am a delivery man and you're a lawyer I am not good enough, huh? Remember we all came from the hood."

"No, that's not the case. Look, where do you want to meet?"

****

Rodney and Kelli decided to meet at the Commander's Palace in uptown New Orleans. It was located across the street from a cemetery in the Garden

District. The area was mostly residential, and the houses' starting prices were about a half of a million dollars. The restaurant was located in a loud green Victorian style house. The third floor was entirely enclosed with glass through which patrons could enjoy a view of the oldest trees in the city.

On the table where Rodney and Kelli were seated were candles and a half empty bottle of Dom Perignon-the second one that they had consumed that evening. Kelli had already polished off a bowl of turtle soup and stuffed crayfish, and a generous portion of Oyster Rockefellers. The dessert would be the banana foster. The chef had already set up a station to prepare it right in front of their eyes. When the liquor was added to the mixture of banana and ice cream, the flames erupted and startled Kelli. Rodney nursed a salad the entire evening.

The night was magical. They reminisced about the good old days-their childhood days when they ran together, days they referred to as the best times of their lives.

"Do you remember the name we used to call ourselves?"

"How could I ever forget, "Money Dawgs." That was the dumbest name for a gang I ever heard."

"Yeah, that was pretty dumb. How did we come up with that anyway?"

"Well, remember Coal used to follow his brother around all the time, and we used to follow Coal around all the time? One day his brother got pissed with Coal and told him to stop following him around like a puppy. And Coal jumped in his brother's face and said, 'I ain't no puppy man, I am a Dawg.' His brother said, 'you ain't shit.' They started fighting and me, you, and Sheena jumped in it too."

"Yeah, now I am starting to remember that stuff. I got my butt kicked big time by Coal's brother. You started crying. Coal went flying across the room. The only one who stayed on him the whole time was Sheena. She wouldn't let go of his back. Coal kept getting up and jumping on him and getting thrown off but Sheena would not let go. Me and you kept doing the same thing. Finally out of sheer aggravation, his brother called him a Dawg, just to make us stop. The rest of us were his Money Dawgs because we were all about making dollars and we stuck so close to him."

They laughed hard about how stupid the name was, and how it became the name of their group from that day forward. Throughout their time at Holy Ghost Catholic school, their gang was Money Dawgs and everybody knew not to fuck with them.

"It's a shame how everybody went their separate ways after grammer school and not keep up with each other. I thought we would have been dawgs for life."

"Well, I still keep up with Coal and Sheena. You are really the only one that has been out of the loop."

"You must really be doing your own thing besides working for Mr. IPS to afford to bring me to a place like this."

She was impressed that Rodney had taken her here, but she began to wonder if he would have enough money to pay the tab. The bill at this point was well over two hundred dollars.

"This is a nice restaurant Rodney. I am surprised and impressed."

"So you didn't think the delivery man had learned a little class did you?"

She teased, "I figured you had some class. I did see you in that fancy car dealership, and I am here ain't I?

"You know I have big dreams too. One day when I come to a place like this they will have a special table for me with my name on it. And all those waiters in the back will know who I am and line up to serve me. The only question will be who I'll share it all with?"

"That is so typical. Why do men think when they're successful they need to have someone there to share it with them? Why can't you just be successful by yourself? Why does success need a mate?" Kelli never wanted anyone special in her life. She was fine with the one night stands and never wanted anything complicated. Once men satisfied her physical and financial needs, she had no use for them.

"It is part of the laws of nature, baby: a king needs a queen, a lion needs a lioness, a man needs a woman."

"Forget that shit. All I need is me. So how do you figure fame and fortune will come to you? No disrespect, but right now you're just a deliveryman."

"Sneakers, my dear, sneakers."

"Tennis shoes?"

"Yeah, I have designed a shoe. The ultimate tennis shoe. It makes you run faster, jump higher. It's called Bullet Tennis Shoes."

"Bullet tennis shoes—interesting. How far along are you on this?"

"The shoe has been designed. It really works."

"Tell me about your delivery job."

Rodney and Kelli continued to talk as the restaurant began to close. Rodney requested a bill at which time a charcoal brother who resembled Rodney came and presented the check.

This is the moment of truth Kelli thought, let see how his ass handles this.

Although she was enjoying the conversation, she still wanted to see if he could really be the big spender type that she usually spent her time with. Still the conversation with Rodney was refreshing, different from the kind she usually spent her time with.Still the conversation with Rodney was refreshing, different from the kind she usually had with men who were only interested in the latest hustle and getting her to bed.

Rodney took the check without hesitation.
"Thanks Cuz, I really appreciate you taking care of me with the family discount. Kelli, meet my cousin Ronald. He is the head bus boy here, and he took care of us big time tonight."

"What's up, sistah? Any friend of Rodney is a friend of mine."

Kelli did not answer, but gave Ronald a knowing smirk. She was pissed. How dare he rely on a discount to take her to a place like this? To her, this was like buying her a present from the Walmart—unacceptable.

Rodney ignored her inhospitable attitude and gave Ronald a fifty-dollar bill wrapped in the check. He stood up and gave Ronald a bear hug before he walked away. Despite Kelli's rudeness, Rodney saw something in Kelli he liked. He remembered her innocence and the crush he had on her when they were kids. He didn't know that Kelli was not the same girl he had known long before.

Kelli had grown into a beautiful women that he was attracted to with more than just his eyes. The bulge in his pants proved that he had a physical attraction to her as well.

"This place is closing, let's go to this hot club on Pine Street. It's called Club D'Plex. Its supposed to be gutter. Lil Wayne and a lot of the Cash Money Rappers hang out in there. Wanna check it out?"

Kelli was still pissed off about the dinner, but when she heard about the possibilities of going to a joint where there might be some big time spenders, she readily agreed. Besides, she was getting horny and she needed to fuck somebody before the end of the night anyway.

At Club D'Plex, the joint was off the wall. The place was jamming and the DJ was mixing it up real good. They were playing a lot of Ludacris, R Kelly and Chingy. Kelli started downing gin and tonics like they were going out of style. They danced into the wee hours of the morning. Although there were no rappers there, the combination of the good music and drinks started to lighten Kelli up. The last song they played was Slow Jamz. Kelli was at the table insisting that she had to go because of work in the morning, but Rodney insisted that they dance to that last song. He pulled her to the dance floor and she acquiesced. The closer Kelli got to Rodney's body, the more excited she became by the smell of his cologne and sweat. She rubbed her body close to his, initiating a grind on his private parts. He was definitely feeling her and allowed his body to rest on hers in time to the beats of the song by Twista, Kanye West and Jamie Foxx. Rodney placed his hand on her back and slowly traced her curves with the soft touch of his fingers. Kelli removed his tucked shirt from his trousers and raced her hands up his chest to feel his hard nipples. Rodney couldn't believe he was getting this type of attention from Kelli on their first date. He wanted her just as bad as she wanted him and he was ecstatic when she asked him to go home with her. He only hesitated when he realized he had to follow her 745 to her house in his Honda Civic.

CHAPTER ELEVEN

KELLI

I could barely drive home with all that alcohol I drank. Damn, I would have fucked him at the club if so many people weren't around. Plus, the ladies room was too damn dirty. I usually didn't take niggas to my crib, but I wanted him bad, and no telling where his broke ass lived. We might have ended up sharing a bed with his mamma in the next room,

All I could say was that I knew he was going to be impressed by my place. I knew it was not the shit he was used to. I lived in Lake Forest Estates in the Eastern part of the city. I had a massive ranch on a 1/2 acre estate. In my crib, there were five bedrooms and four baths, and I had a fully equipped gym that would rival Bally's. There was a theatre room with reclining chairs that vibrated heat at the touch of a switch and a 62-inch screen TV. My sofas were covered with mink and my dining room table was Italian marble. And once he saw the bedroom, all he was going to want to do was drop his drawers. My comforter was white silk, and the bed frame and the dressers were made of oak.

I held onto his hand as we walked into the house together. Look at him, I thought, he was trying to seem all cool, but I could tell he was ready to shit on himself. He just kept staring at my antique vase.

"My dear, your place is lovely."

Lovely my ass, I thought, my place was the bomb and he knew it. The African art in this bad boy alone cost over 100 grand.

Fuck that, I am ready to get busy anyway. I pulled him towards me. At the same time he grabbed my other hand and placed it on the upper part of his chest. Rodney began to stare deeply at me. It gave me the creeps though because I thought I could see real affection in his eyes. I kept telling myself this was only for the dick, but my head was just not obeying. His hand on my chest was making me weak. I wanted to get down to just having sex, but he was slowing me down, like we were newlyweds about to engage in lovemaking. He grabbed my hair while passionately kissing me on the lips. His lips caused mine to reciprocate and I opened my mouth to allow him to enter with his tongue. I hadn't gotten the zipper halfway down when his manhood popped out of his Meoshe jeans. I guided him to the sofa and gently pulled off his pants and boxers, revealing his rock hard brown statue.

"Just wait." I told him as I ran to the kitchen to grab some whip cream, strawberries, and a knife.

His penis was still hard when I returned. I didn't know if it was the alcohol, but I wanted to enjoy every minute of him, and the idea of eating him became so appealing. I sprayed the whip cream on him and cut the strawberries right on top of him. I began to suck up the whip cream off of him with the finely cut pieces of strawberry. By the time I was finished, his dick was clean and I was wet and ready to jump on top of him. I pulled off my pants and panties in one sweeping move and jumped on top of him to ride him like a cowgirl. I worked my hips fast and furious. Too furiously. I had to admit that the feel of him inside me made me come in record time. He, however, was still rock hard. He flipped me on top of him and started ramming into me from behind,with me still on top. I couldn't take it. I came again. He was still rock hard. He then flipped me on my hardwood floor and entered me doggy style. I came again. This time the orgasm was even more intense. He was still rock hard. Shit, this was too much for even me to take. He flipped me again and began to enter my mouth with his tongue as his body entered mine. He was slow and gentle, and although I had already come three times, I wanted more of this man. We kissed passionately with the longest wet kisses that I had ever experienced This time we both came together with me screaming at the top of my lungs. Rodney definitely had to stick around awhile.

CHAPTER TWELVE

SHEENA

Our shit was the bomb. Clarence and I went out on that first date, and we had been screwing ever since. The first date at Coplin's was amazing. The food was spicy and I was getting hot just talking to this fine brother. I told Clarence about my background growing up, but I failed to mention my true occupation. I told him I was a copier sales person, I worked out of town a lot, that my salary was based on commission and that I sold a lot of copiers. I know it sounds kinda lame, but how else could I explain my Mercedes 550, my closet full of designer clothes and my slamming apartment in Metairie, an upper

class area neighborhood in the suburb complete with a
doorman? When I brought him there he was so
impressed that you could see Lake Ponchatrain from my
front window. I think Clarence was impressed with my
hood upbringing because he had never dated a ghetto girl
before. I tried to talk properly when I was around him,
but when I said some slang he just smiled.

Well, the man enjoyed wild sex and I provided it
for him. He couldn't get enough of it. Although he was
well equipped, both long and wide, he would bring various medical instruments to my apartment to enhance our
pleasure as we made love. I will never look at a specu-
lum, clamp, or a stethoscope the same again. He also
brought the drugs that kept us high. I never used street
drugs because I had witnessed first hand how that could
bring you down quicker than a heartbeat. In my line of
work, I had to stay physically fit to take care of business
if things got rough or if I had to make a quick escape. At
first I did not want to take the drugs, but Clarence insisted,

"This is going to make you come more intensely
and quickly. Unlike the street drugs, you will never get
addicted to this stuff." His eyes seemed sincere as he said
it, but there was also a hint of impatience. I figured that
if a doctor was taking them too, it had to be okay.

"Take it, trust me." He handed me a glass of

water.

"Now close your eyes and let me massage you."

"Are you going to take some?"

"I already had mine at work."

Clarence's hands gently reached up my blouse and massaged my chest. My nipples grew stiff at the touch of his hand. I lay on the sofa. He cuddled, caressed and smothered my breast with his smooth gentle hands. He continued to massage them with one hand as he unbuttoned my shirt. His lips felt like honey when they touched my skin. A cold chill swept over my body, and I began to shiver. I wasn't sure if it was the drugs or his touch, that made my head spin. He sucked on my nipples like he was trying to get the last drop out of a soda bottle with a straw. It didn't hurt when he put the clamp into me. My reaction made him smile. I was wondering how I didn't feel any pain with something the size of that instrument inside me. He pulled it out and it was bloody, which turned him on more. He thrusted his stiff shaft into me and rammed it fast and hard.

"Shit, this stuff is good," I screamed after experiencing the most intense orgasm of my life. He still kept coming, and the thrust of his dick was so hard I thought the tip of his penis had reached my throat.

I never thought anything was wrong with the drugs Clarence brought to the apartment after that.

I only saw him a few times a week since he explained that he spent most of his time at the hospital. When I asked him about his apartment, he said that it was being renovated, and he was ashamed of its current condition. The only way I could contact him was with his cell phone because he said he didn't have a land line since he was never home. I never questioned anything he said because I knew doctors worked all the time, and shit, I was falling in love with him. I dreamed of marrying Clarence and settling down with him. I even imagined having his babies. He introduced me to the prospect of a different life. Maybe I could get out of the ghetto. The thrill of the kill no longer excited me; only Clarence's body could do that for me now.

Clarence treated me well, and he made me feel like a real woman. I told him about my father. He didn't laugh or make fun, and he was even sympathetic.

Larry did die eventually, as my targets always do, but because of my relationship with Clarence, I didn't want to go on being a hit woman. I knew it wasn't the type of occupation I could hold if I wanted a future with him. I started to think about some legitimate business to get into. The problem was that I didn't have any other skills. I had a black belt in karate from Master Lee. I had firearm training, and judo training. I went to the gym every day to work out. I had trained to be a master killer, and there wasn't too many other businesses that required killer skills. On the other hand, money was not a problem. I had made enough with my hits to invest in a business.

Coal was tripping when I told him I was going to stop doing hits and go legit. He laughed and said I loved this shit too much to stop. He was constantly making enemies and really didn't have anyone as proficient as me making hits. He knew because of our history, that I was smart enough not to get caught, and even if I did, I would never turn on him. He also commented on my weight loss and how tired I looked.

"Are you trying to look like one of those skinny blond whores for your fancy doctor? What's the deal?"

"Mind your own business. I am telling you now I am quitting."

"Look, Sheena, I need you to do more for me. I don't have anyone who can handle business like you."

"Sorry, Coal. I am out. You are a big boy now, and you can handle it yourself."

All I knew was that I loved Clarence, and I would do anything to spend my life with him.

CHAPTER THIRTEEN

RODNEY

Rodney walked into the IPS warehouse and noticed that his work area was surrounded by flowers. He was also sporting a new Movado watch.

"Man, this is impressive. Real impressive. So you're that good?" his buddy asked.

"Today watches, tomorrow tennis shoes."

Rodney's mother was cleaning his house when the door bell rang. Rodney's mother opened the door to see a man with flowers.

"For me?"

"Rodney Walker?

Rodney's mother took the vase and the package and brought them over to the phone. She picked up the receiver and dialed Rodney's number.

"Rodney, I was cleaning your house and this man came to the door and left these beautiful flowers and a box."

"Yeah."

"You must have someone real special to send you these nice things."

"Yeah, real special. Later Ma."

Rodney put his finger on the receiver and dialed Kelli's number.

"I want to thank you for sending me the flowers and gift."

"Did you like it?"

"I love it, but I haven't seen it yet. My mama was home when it came in."

"You mean you live with your mother?"

"No, it's not that. She cleans my house for me occasionally."

"I see; a mama's boy." she said teasingly.

"No, it is not that. She just cleans up. Come over to my house tonight and I'll cook for you."

"I don't know, I am kind of swamped with work."

"No excuses. See you at 7."

Rodney didn't really want to invite Kelli to his

house. He was ashamed of his crib compared to Kelli whose crib was so nice it could have been on the next edition of that MTV Cribs show. However, he was starting to fall in love with her again. He knew he had loved her in grammar school but as the years flew by so did his feelings. They were definitely back now. He could sense that the years had changed her as well. She was no longer the innocent schoolgirl that he'd shared his feelings with. She had toughened up over the years, and he felt that a lot of her innocence was lost. Was this the lawyer part of her that corrupted the girl she was once to the woman she was today. If they had a future together she had to find out about him. One day, with his sneakers, he would make the type of money she made and more. For now, she just had to appreciate the man he was, that would be his test for her.

CHAPTER FOURTEEN

RODNEY

Rodney and Kelli were getting comfortable at Rodney's house. Rodney was stirring a big pot of file gumbo that he had been working on for about an hour. He had just added the crabs that were as big as his fist. The crabs were alive and Rodney was careful that the claws didn't grab a piece of his fingers.

"The last thing I am going to add are the shrimps and we'll be ready to eat. The chicken and the potato salad are already ready."

Kelli had a wine glass in her hand and was look-ing around Rodney's house. She noticed the books on his shelf in the room next to the kitchen. Rodney's house was small but clean. There were only about five rooms in the house, including the bathroom and a small kitchen.

Damn, I got more bedrooms in my house than he has rooms in this shack, Kelle thought.

Kelli observed the hanging tennis shoes and drawings of sneakers on the wall.

"You are really into this Bullet tennis shoe thing, aren't you?"

"Sure am. I am going to make a fortune. These sneakers are designed better than Nike, Adidas, and Air Jordan all combined."

Rodney walked over to the shoe on his desk. "Looka here, these shoes have what I call the ultra design, anyone who wears these runs faster, jumps higher."

While Rodney went on about the sneakers, Kelli noticed Rodney's company invoice sitting on one of his shelves. She looked at it and smiled.

Kelli came behind Rodney and started nibbling the back of his neck causing an arousal in his passion. Rodney turned her around and looked her straight into her eyes.

"You're different from the Kelli I knew back in the day. What got you to turn so cold?"

"What, you don't think I'm treating you right? I have given you nice things haven't I? I have satisfied all your needs, haven't I?"

"Baby, you are the best thing that has happened to me in a long time. You don't have to give me gifts, I don't care about material things. I care about you and I feel in your heart there is something troubling you."

"You want to know about my past since we were in school?"

"Yeah, I want to know everything about you."

Kelli was impressed. It has been a long time since she was with a man who wanted to know about her.

"I was married once, for a short time. My husband went to prison after we were married three years. He had this problem, selling drugs, he was busted and was going to get 15 years."

"So, he is in jail now."

"No, he's dead."

"Dead?"

"Prison never became him. He tried to cut a deal with the State against his supplier to cut his time. They got to him in prison and killed him."

"He couldn't just do the fifteen."

"No, he wanted to get out fast; he had his reasons."

Kelli turned away from Rodney, tears in her eyes.

"I lost my mother the same year, so it was rough for a while. After he went to jail, I took a job with the law office I work for now." Rodney pulled Kelli close.

"I can tell you loved him. I'm here for you."

Rodney led her to the kitchen table and guided her to the chair. "I am hungry, I am ready to eat."

He opened a cabinet and grabbed a bowl that he filled with gumbo and placed in front of Kelli. The wine had made Kelli extremely hungry, so she hurriedly lapped down the gumbo. Rodney just watched. When she looked up, she saw his stare with a hungry look in his eyes.

"You are not going to eat?"

"I need some ice first."

He opened the freezer and placed an ice cube between his teeth. He pushed Kelli's chair back from the kitchen table and rolled her long black skirt to her waist revealing red silk thongs. Since it was so hot all the time in New Orleans, Kelli rarely wore stockings. Rodney grabbed each thong by the side and pulled her panties down to her knees. He immediately slipped his big firm hands under her bra and began to stroke them. The ice between his teeth was immediately applied to her vagina where he proceeded to rub it fast and furiously. Kelli head flew back in ecstasy.

"That feels good." She could barely get the words out of her mouth. The combination of her cold pussy and the massaging of her breast caused Kelli to feel a sensation like no other. She came like a firecracker, howling her pleasure loud enough for the neighbors to hear her from the small house.

"Damm, that was good."

Rodney's face appeared from between her legs. He licked his lips.

"Now, let me show you why I really like gumbo."

Rodney grabbed a bowl and placed some hot steamy gumbo in it. He resumed the position under the table. There he took a swallow of the gumbo juice and placed his warm tongue on her clit. He repeated it until the warm juices ran down her body and she tasted like gumbo. Now it was his turn to lap up the gumbo like a dog. He held her opened legs tight and licked her vigorously, his tongue moving faster and faster like a man who hadn't eaten in days. It was tough for Kelli to come so soon after the first one, so she begged him to stop. Rodney ignored her pleads and began to gently bite her clit causing her more pleasure. He wouldn't stop until his mission was complete. He wanted her to come again and despite the fact she was hitting his head for him to stop, he continued. He ate her for at least ten minutes. Kelli decided that resistance was futile and just relaxed her body. This time when she screamed, her body became lifeless. Rodney raised his head again with a smile, his faced covered with cream.

He led her exhausted, to the bedroom and placed her on the bed. He slowly undressed her. She noticed the bulge in his pants.

"Rodney, I need some energy after that. I don't think I can go again."

"That's all right, I'll take care of you."

He went to the kitchen and dished her a plate of fried chicken and potato salad. Rodney brought the plate to the bedroom and delicately fed her the chicken and salad with a fork.

"You know I am gonna make you love me. I can take care of you like no other man could."

She took the plate out of his hand and began to unbutton his shirt. She passionately kissed him on the lips. He in turn allowed his tongue to explore her mouth. He then proceeded to kiss her on the face as his hand caressed her breasts.

Kelli grabbed his belt and forced her hand down his pants without unloosening it. She used her other hand to spring his manhood open. He leaped on top of her and immediately pumped himself into her opened legs. After their lovemaking, they both fell into a deep sleep. Kelli woke before Rodney and began dressing quietly, careful not to wake him. She snuck back into the room where she saw Rodney's company invoice and slipped that into her pocket with a big smile.

Rodney woke to find her gone and smiled when he saw the package on the pillow that Kelli had left him.

S.W. Smith

CHAPTER FIFTEEN

SHEENA

Clarence kept me waiting all night for him. He didn't even call until about 2a.m. Said he was in emergency surgery. I didn't know he was a surgeon. I just thought he was a regular doctor. Clarence and I haven't been spending too much time together lately. We had been together for one year and I was ready to go on the next level with our relationship. I got my business going. I bought rental property and now collected rent on seven properties. Even on the nights he was not working at the hospital, he said he was too tired to come over. I asked him to go to the Bayou Classic: the football game where Southern and Grambling Universities played every year at the Superdome the weekend after Thanksgiving. During halftime, they have a Battle of the Bands show between the two schools that was worth the ticket price alone. I surprised him with front row seats. He looked happy to get the tickets, but he said he couldn't go because he had to work. The tickets went to waste. Come to think of it, he never spent his birthday or any holidays with me. He always said he had to work.

I was looking forward to going on a cruise with him to Cancun Mexico that weekend. It would be a chance for us to relax and spend some quality time together. I loved Clarence, but lately he had just been coming over for a short time, having a little sex and leaving. We used to cuddle up for hours after making love, but we didn't do that anymore. He was too busy at the hospital. The boat left on Friday afternoon and returned Sunday evening. I had been telling him about the cruise for about eight weeks. I got all my new outfits ready and packed. Clarence called and said that he would meet me at the ship and he would bring all the goodies. I reminded him jokingly that the boat left at 5p.m. with or without him, confident of our upcoming good time together.

At 4:30p.m., I was at the entrance to the ship waiting for Clarence. My cell phone rang. He said he had an emergency at the hospital again and that I would have to go without him. Heartbroken, I entered the ship, determined to have a good time anyway. The only problem was, I didn't have Clarence or the drugs he was supposed to bring.

Three days on that boat gave me time to clear my head. I needed clarity in my relationship with Clarence, and I needed it then. I looked in the mirror. My once full face was thin, and my skin was clinging to my bones. I had given up my lucrative occupation for him, and now I was hooked on drugs, and barely seeing him. After each encounter, the pleasure I felt immediately turned to pain. I had even started to take drugs to control the pain. My insides felt raw. I had to regain the control I once had over my life.

When the ship docked, I knew what needed to be done. I had to find out what was going on with Clarence. I left the boat and immediately drove to his home. Even though I had never been there, I always knew where he lived in the garden district of uptown New Olreans. I drove around until I had located the house that matched the address I found on the internet. It was a beautiful house: three stories, freshly painted. There was even a swing on the porch dancing in the wind. I pulled up closer to the curb and waited. I didn't have to wait long. Through the shades, I could see the shadows of two people. A man and a woman. I got out of the car to get a better view.

The lights of the house went out, and I could no longer see inside. I went back to the car to get the gun I always kept in the glove compartment. I hurriedly ran back to the house. I crept in the back door and up to the master bedroom. They were getting down in the bed in front of me. I stood transfixed on their actions. Unlike with me, Clarence was gentle with this woman. He slowly and carefully came in and out of her. Nowhere in sight were the medical tools he used on me. I became outraged. I pulled out the gun I held and fired two shots: one in the back of Clarence's head, and one in the woman's forehead. Instead of getting out of there, I just screamed and cried. I couldn't move. All the emotions I had never experienced with killing and death, even with my father's death, came pouring out of me. I became hysterical.

Somebody must have heard the shots, (my dumb ass hadn't remembered to use the silencer that time) because the police sure got there quickly. I was arrested and brought down to Central Lockup on Broad Street. The charge was double murder, and no bond was set. This was some fucked up shit. Of all the people I had aced, I got caught getting emotionally involved with some mutherfucka who had used me the fuck up. Within 24 hours, I was brought to the magistrate court where I pleaded not guilty. My bond remained the same. Word got out quickly about the shooting. It was all over the newspapers and TV, since Clarence was a promising doctor at Charity Hospital. I found out that the girl with him was a sister of a gang leader, Chico, the head of the Jungle Brothers. She was a civilian and was employed as a teacher. The biggest shock to me was that the woman was Clarence's wife. He was playing me from day one. All those excuses about working 24 hour shifts, and he was at home with his wifey.

Being in jail got me real nervous. Once I found out who Clarence's wife was, I knew there would be trouble. There was no way Chico was going to let his sister's death go unavenged.

I didn't have the money to hire a real attorney because it was all tied up in the real estate that I bought, so I was appointed a public defender. Kelli claimed she had a heavy caseload and didn't have the time to devote to my case. Bitch, I knew she was all about money and because I didn't have any, fuck the friendship, she wasn't gettin' involved. It was a shame cause I know she could beat this with no problem. I knew Coal wouldn't help me at this point because I refused to do that last hit for him.

I complained to the public defender about the need of getting out of jail and she said she would do her best to have the charges reduced to manslaughter and get a bond set, since I was in love with Clarence. She indicated though it would take some time to do this. I told her I didn't have that time because of Clarence's wife connection to the gang. If I stayed there, I knew I would be dead sooner rather than later. She said she would get me in a separate cell in an isolated unit in the meantime.

I was glad to hear that. The tension at the prison was getting thick. Other women in prison had approached me and tested me already. This bitch approached me as I was shooting some hoops in the yard and indicated she was going to kick my ass for playing on her court. She attempted to punch me; I ducked and gave her an ass kicking of her life. Two blows: one to her head, the other to her neck and she went down. I walked away before the sheriffs got there to see who was doing the fighting.

My roommate was another issue. She didn't say a word to me. Just stared. I asked her all the time what the fuck she looking at, and she didn't say a word. I knew she was plotting on me, waiting until I slipped up. I hadn't really slept well since I'd been here. I had to sleep with one eye open, just in case. I sat up in my bed and covered myself with pillows in case an attack came at night. I didn't know how much longer I could do this. I didn't know what was worst, the lack of sleep or just being in here. That lawyer had better get me outta here quickly or I was sure the worse was yet to come. I would rather be dead than be holed up in a place like this.

CHAPTER SIXTEEN

KELLI

I really was getting fond of Rodney. He definitely knew how to lay down the pipe. Too bad his ass was broker than the Ten Commandments or I might have permanently hooked up with him. Well, back to the practice of law. Let's see I have a 12'oclock with a Mr. Black. I wonder what that is about.

"Silvia, when Mr. Black gets in, please let me know. "

"He's already in, I will escort him in."

My secretary Silvia had a big smile on her face when she let in Mr. Black, but he looked like one big mean dude. Don't get me wrong, he was a dark chocolate, muscular, good looking brother with a fine body and wavy hair, but something about the look on his face let me know immediately he wasn't one to be fucked with. Shit, he had the word Killer tattooed on that big arm of his with a picture of a gun on top of it. Talk about conspicuous, that MF must get stopped five times a day by the police. Still, with that body I bet he must be a wild man in bed. I was gonna have to get some of that.

"Have a seat, Mr. Black. My secretary said you called about an appointment for a criminal matter. I presume you have been falsely charged, and you want the best lawyer money can buy, so you called me."

"I am here on a criminal matter, but I haven't been charged with anything yet."

"Yet, so you want some advice on what to do if charged?"

"No, I am not here for that either."

"Then what is a good looking brother like you here for?" I asked with a big toothy grin.

He didn't crack a smile or bat an eye. "I am here to get the money you stole from my brother."

"Excuse me, I don't know what you are talking about."

"I'll tell you what the fuck I am talking about. You represented my brother Ricky Charles six months ago in federal court on a possession of coke with intent to distribute. He pled guilty and got fifteen years. According to you, he woulda got 25 years, but you told him that if he turned over the money he had stashed from drug sales he would only get fifteen. My brother told you the money was in a suitcase in Atlanta at my grandmother's house and you said you would pick it up."

"Yeah, I remember your brother. I did drive to Atlanta, picked up the suitcase and turned it over to the feds and your brother got fifteen years. So?"

"Bitch! You think people stupid! He had $200,000.00 in that suitcase, when you turned in the suitcase it only had $100,000.00. What the fuck happened to the other 100 grand?"

"Man, I don't know what you are talking about. When I picked up the suitcase it had a lock on it, and I turned it in the same way."

"Don't play with me. All you had to do was cut the lock and put another lock on the suitcase. Now I am only gonna ask you one more time. Where is the rest of the money?"

Black moved closer to my desk after he made his last statement in a heated voice. I had to think quickly on this one. I didn't know if he had a gun on him, but I wouldn't have put it past him. Fuck, I didn't know Charles had a brother. On top of that, I didn't think they would have missed the money, especially since I put the exact same lock on the suitcase.

I eased out of my chair and slowly approached Black with the most innocent look I could muster. I sat on his lap and put my hand on his hair. By the feel of the bulge on his lap, this brother was definitely packing.

With the most sweetness I could muster I whispered in his ear as I played with his hair, "I promise you I didn't steal anything from your brother. What was in the suitcase when I got it went straight to the federal prosecutor who opened it. It could have been him or someone at your grandmother's house who took the money, I certainly didn't."

Thump!

That was the sound of my butt hitting the floor after Black pushed me off his lap.

He jumped on top of me and raised his fist as if he were going to knock me out right then and there. His other hand pulled me up by my hair. Only then did I see the gun in his waistband. I was too afraid to scream.

"Slut, you have a week to get me the money or you are one dead bitch."

I was so afraid of him at that point I blurted out, "Look, I will get you your money, but I need at least four weeks."

"Tell you what, I will give you four weeks to come up with $200,000.00. Consider that as payment in full with interest. Now if you go to the police I will kill you before they even have a chance to catch up with me. Besides, if the police finds out you skimmed off the money, you are going to jail anyway. So it is your decision, death or jail."

Tears begin to flow from my eyes. "Whatever, I will get you your money."

His hand let go of my hair and he stroked my wet jaw.

"Aw, don't cry, if you get the money earlier than the four weeks I will let you finish up that lap dance you started on me. You know I was getting a little excited." Then he smiled a big toothy grin.

Black turned his back and walked out of my office leaving me on the floor. I put my hand on my face and I wondered what the fuck was I thinking about when I bought that marble dining room set with Ricky's money.

I got up to get myself together for my next client whom I knew from prior dealings. Actually, I had summoned him to my office because I figured I could make some money off of some of the old clients he had.

Kevin Washington was a former hustler who had previously supplied Algiers section of New Orleans. He dealt coke and had about three hundred and fifty people he was supplying. How did I know that? When his butt was busted by the cops, the stupid MF he was had a database on his computer of all his customers that the police seized. The only way I got him off was by a technicality, illegal search by the police since they didn't have the probable cause to search the computer when the only thing he had in his house was a dime bag of marijuana.

The rest of his drugs, 94 Kilos in the form of large bricks were set for delivery the same night the police raided him. They came in too soon and never got the rest of the evidence. Kevin was so grateful that I saved him from life in prison, he pledged his undying gratitude to me in addition to a nice legal fee that nearly drained his bank account. However, he swore he was out of the game because he came so close to spending life in jail and he had a son he had to watch out for. I could appreciate that but what I needed was his customer list and his supplier. I had distribution worked out in my mind and I was planning to make a bit hit and retire from the practice. The way I figured it, I could make about ten million dollars in a short period of time and quit practicing. Don't get me wrong. I made a nice living in the law business but nothing like the money that I had seen my hustling clients make. Now it seemed like I had no choice with Mr. Black on my tail.

"Kevin, how are you? Have a seat, man; I need your help bad."

"What's up counselor? You know I will do anything to help my lawyer."

"I need the backup list of your clients and your product connections."

"Hold on. I said I would do anything to help my lawyer but there are limits. I am not putting myself in a position to do time for nobody."

"I am not asking you to put yourself in any type of position that would harm you. All I need is the information. Remember the floppy disk that the police didn't seize with your backup client list that you said you had after your bust and the name of your supplier. I will take care of the distribution my damn self. Or maybe you are not as grateful as you said you were. You told me a lot about your past. And I know now you are a straight up guy. You know attorney client privilege is the damnest thing. Not that I would do it, but there have been some lawyers who have quietly dropped a dime on their clients, letting the cops know of all kinds of stuff their clients were involved in. You know I would never do that to you, but I need your help here, and I want you to show me some appreciation for saving your butt."

"Enough. I can give you the disk, but my connection is gone. Once I got busted I told them I was out of the game. Plus, they were afraid that I dropped a dime on them to get out. So, in other words, they ain't gonna deal with me no more."

I saw the desperation in Kevin's eyes and I knew he was telling the truth. It made sense for his supplier not to deal with him again.

"Okay, don't sweat it, have the disk here by tomorrow and we are even."

"Counselor, you are playing a dangerous game, I hope you know what you are doing."

"Damn skippy man. I can play this game better than my clients. There is more than one supplier out there. One other thing I need you to do for me."

I walked behind him and locked the door to the office. In one motion, I massaged the back of his neck as I saddled his legs. I quickly begin to unbutton his shirt.

"I remembered when I represented you, you knew exactly how to take care of a sistah. You still have those skills."

"Yea, I can still hook a sistah up." Kevin began kissing on my breast.

Well, he ain't as big as I imagined Black would be, but as horny as I was, he would have to do.

CHAPTER SEVENTEEN

RODNEY

"Baby, I left something in your car. Can I see your keys?"

"Sure, sweetie, they are on the counter."

Kelli took the keys from the counter and got into Rodney's car. She was immediately turned off by it. Damn, I hope no one sees me in this wreck. At least he could try to pimp his ride. I'm gonna have to drop a line to that Pimp My Ride show about this wreck because this is too nasty. From now on I drive my own car. Bad enough I had to get high last night just to get in the shit. I've got enough stuff, Coal won't miss it.

She drove the car to the 24-hour convenience store down the street. On the window there was a huge sign that read Keys Made. Kelli handed the IPS truck key to the clerk who made a copy for her. She got back into Rodney's car and drove to her house. She walked over to her car and took a package out of her trunk and placed it into Rodney's trunk. When Kelli got back to Rodney's house, she put the package into the IPS truck. She went to the cab portion of the truck and placed a duplicate invoice sheet at the bottom of a stack on a clipboard that contained the delivery address of her package. Kelli slipped quickly in the house and got back onto the bed.

"I was getting kinda lonely. What took you so long?"

"I hope you didn't mind I had to run back to my house to get some clean clothes. Lately I have been spending so much time here I feel like I have been moving in."

"I love the fact that you are here for me. I don't want it any other way." He hugged her closer to him.

They embraced for a long period of time as he planted his long juicy tongue down her mouth. They began passionate love making again and were interrupted by the alarm clock ringing to the hour of seven.

Rodney panted, "Baby, I gotta go to work." He tried to pull himself away as Kelli resisted. "Baby, if I didn't know better I would think you were a nymphomaniac. You never get enough."

Kelli laughed, "You are the only one I can't get enough of."

"Well, we'll have to finish this tonight. Until my sneaker thing takes off, I gotta keep this job. Can I drop you off at your house?"

Kelli thought, Hell no; this time of day I am liable to be seen in that piece of shit.

But she thought better, than to say it. Sure, baby, you can drop me off, and I will see you tonight after work.

$$

Unbeknownst to Rodney for the next four weeks he continued to deliver packages for Kelli. Kelli continued to duplicate the delivery sheets adding her own packages sometimes as many as twenty a day. She would meet Rodney at his house in the evenings and transfer the packages from her trunk to his truck once he would fall asleep after their heavy tryst of lovemaking. Rodney was never the wiser. The packages contained different quantities of cocaine to Kevin's old clientele. She had gotten Kevin to let them know she would be their supplier, but they would have to come to her law office to prepay for the shipment. The payments would be made in cash directly to her, but she would give them a receipt for legal services. Because they had to wait a day for delivery, she would give them lagniappe or extra product. If they talked to her about anything other than law related issues, they would be immediately dropped from the list of clientele. Kelli knew that any other conversation could be a trap so she decided she would not talk to them about anything else but legal services which, was the buzz word for drugs. The amount of drugs the person wanted would be described as the amount of time spent on a legal case. For instance, 2 pounds of coke would be charged as ten hours of legal services, and the client would be given a receipt for 10 hours at $250.00 an hour. Kelli was raking in $50,000.00 per week. Since she had to pay Black and Coal, she knew she had to bring it up a notch.

CHAPTER EIGHTEEN

SHEENA

The lawyer finally came through and got me into an isolated cell. Only problem was, the section they put me in was the section where some of the worst offenders were housed. Every mutherfucka in there had a conviction for murder. What the fuck! At least I didn't have to worry about a roommate.

Although she was a petite Latino girl with blond hair who bore a resemblance to Carmeron Diaz, the lawyer seemed to be pretty good. She came to visit me a lot and talked to me about the case. She said she had her heart broken before by her first love so she knew exactly what I was going through. She said when it happened to her she felt like killing the mug too, but she decided instead to channel her anger and to go to law school.

She only had a little experience, but she said she was going to start a private practice any day now because she thought that was the way for her to make her some real money.

I told her if she got me out of this mess, I would help her build her practice since I was connected in the right ways. I even mentioned how tight I was with Coal. It didn't seem to phase her one bit. She said she had some of her own connections that she was working on and that it wouldn't be a problem starting her own practice.

I was real happy with the way she handled my defense. She showed me a stack of papers that she called discovery requests, which questioned the prosecutors on the type of case they had against me. She also requested a preliminary examination in which she had an opportunity to question some of the people they intended to call as witnesses.

They put the officer who arrested me on the stand, and, let me tell you, it was on like a neck bone. She asked him whether he had probable cause to arrest me since no one actually saw me do the shooting.

My attorney yelled, "Since you didn't see my

client pull the trigger, you really don't know if she came in and found the gun and the bodies after someone else shot the victims."

"I wouldn't say that."

She had the officer so unsure of himself on the stand, I was beginning to believe I was innocent. She continued to grill him like a hungry tiger after a piece of meat. I was impressed, and I knew I was in good hands..

CHAPTER NINETEEN

KELLI

I have got to make more money quicker. Maybe I could let Rodney know what was going on, cut him in, and get him to increase the number of packages he delivered. Damn, he was just too goody goody to let him know what was going on. There were two things I knew I could use to get him to work with me.

Outside the Grandiose Boarding School, my 10-year old Tisha ran out to greet me. She had the suitcase and was ready to spend spring break with me. I hadn't seen her in about 4 months because she had been away in boarding school. I didn't get much of a chance to visit her because I was so busy, but I really missed her.

I gave her a big hug. "The only one Mommie loves."

We got into my car and drove to Rodney's. I told Tisha to stay in the car while I went into Rodney's place since I needed to convince him to help me.

"I have a surprise for you."

Rodney pulled me towards him and started kissing and undressing me in the doorway. I pushed him and turned away.

"Wait, wait. Tisha, come here."

Rodney stopped and stared as Tisha came out of the car and ran toward me with a big grin across her face.

"This is my daughter, Tisha."

"Daughter?"

"Yes, my daughter."

Rodney extended his hand to Tisha. "Your daughter is my daughter."

"Rodney, that is so sweet." I looked into his eyes. "Now I know why I love you."

I could see that Rodney was taken aback by my statement as he pulled me closer to hug me. Pretty soon I was going to have him wrapped around my little finger.

CHAPTER TWENTY

RODNEY

The man and woman sitting inside the Crown Victoria observed Kelli, Rodney, and Tisha and found it quite amusing. They were FBI agents, Carolyn Walker and Abram King and they had begun following Kelli recently. They knew she was distributing drugs, but they didn't have enough evidence to bring her in. They picked up Kevin on a probation violation and he spelled out in detail how the lawyer was distributing product. Because of Kevin's priors, his testimony would be useless in court, so now they had to sit and wait.

"Look how nice, she brought the kid to see this

sap."

"Yeah, this sucker is so lame. He doesn't know what he has gotten into."

"Should we pick him up now."

"Naw, let him dig the hole deeper, then he will have no choice but to cooperate with us."

$$\$$$

The next week, Rodney and Kelli were in front of a loan officer signing papers for Rodney's bank loan. Kelli had cosigned for him, enabling him to get the money. They left the bank and went directly to a warehouse that Rodney had leased where men were bringing in equipment and office furniture. There were boxes all over the floor of the warehouse. Rodney had already gotten a shipment of sneakers from Taiwan. The bullet emblems were on to tables all around the warehouse waiting to be sewn to the sneakers.

Kelli wrapped her arm around Rodney's chest.

"Baby, your stuff is bad. I know it is only a matter of time before you sell more sneakers than Michael Jordan."

"I owe everything to you. I don't know how I am ever gonna repay you, but I would like to spend the rest of my life trying."

"Don't worry, baby, I am sure I can think of something. We'll talk tonight. I gotta go, so I will see you later." She placed a big wet smack on his lips before she walked out of the door.

Rodney immediately grabbed the sneakers and called the Taiwan factory to give them more specifications on the shoe. After staying on the phone for about a half hour, he decided to go out for a minute to get a breath of fresh air.

He was accosted by Walker and King once he hit the front door. They lifted` their badges for his view. They grabbed Rodney by both arms, directing him toward their car.

"I am agent Walker, and this is agent King. We need to ask you a few questions."

"Obviously, you have a case of mistaken identity here, cuz I am just a businessman, and I don't know what questions of yours I could possibly answer."

"Just shut the fuck up until we get in the car."

They shoved him to the back seat of their car where they began their interrogation.

King started. "You know your high priced lawyer girlfriend ain't nothing but a coke dealer."

"I don't know what the fuck you are talking about."

"Don't play dumb with me. You know exactly what I am talking about. "

"I don't know jack, but I do know the number of my high priced lawyer who will make sure you lose your jobs over harassing and insulting a tax paying business-man."

Walker patiently responded. "Let me tell you a story about a lawyer. She struggles through law school and right after graduation meets a man who treats her to all the finer things in life. Too bad he is one of the biggest dealers in East New Orleans. She falls in love with him, gets pregnant, then marries him after the baby is born. He helps her set up her practice and hooks her up to all the hustlers in the game who she represented. They have a big house, nice cars and boats and he treats her and her daughter well. Unfortunately, the good times end when he gets busted and is sentenced to real jail time. Her busi-ness starts to dry up, and life is not as good as it used to be. So she decides to carry on the family business. She uses her new boyfriend to make deliveries when distribu-tion is slow. He is so puppy ass in love with her, he deliv-ers her packages, no questions asked."

Walker leaned forward and gently placed her hand on Rodney's shoulder. "How do you like my story?"

"I don't. It's complete bullshit."

"You don't? Huh, I am not surprised. What is still a question for me is did you know that you were delivering drug?"

"Hell no!"

"I bet if we went in your truck right now we'd have a couple of kilos packed for delivery. The problem is if we bust you now we don't get the big fish we want, including your girlfriend."

Rodney was in disbelief. This shit can't be happening after the opening of my sneaker factory. This is some ill stuff. I knew my delivery schedule was always over booked, but I had been so busy with the sneakers and Kelli, I didn't bother checking at work.

"I don't care if you rot in jail. You have the chance to set this straight. I see you like to make tennis shoes. You have to work with us if you want to be able to continue selling those Air Rodneys you've been making."

"Yeah, we checked you out. We know you have a clean background and been working steadily. That is the reason why we are willing to help you."

"Thanks, but no thanks. It ain't that kind of party. I am not going to sell anybody out."

"Kinda hasty decision for someone who is about

to lose their life's dream and spend a lot of time in jail. Who knows, maybe there is a big market for sneakers in the inmate population? How long have you wanted to own a sneaker factory? How many years of sweat have you put into this?"

Walker raised Rodney's foot to look at the sneaker. "Man, those are some nice sneaks. I can see Jay-Z endorsing them now. I know you don't have anything to do with this drug thang, but don't make me bring you down for it. Somebody has to go down, so it can be you or the people really responsible for it."

"I need some time to think about this. Real time."

"We are only giving you three days; then we shut you down."

King pulled Rodney out of the car. "Make sure you don't deliver the packages left in your truck."

They drove off as Rodney crossed the street to get to his truck. He hadn't quit IPS yet, thinking that he would wait until the orders for his sneakers started flowing in. Besides, Kelli was always telling him not to quit until he was sure his business would succeed, and that could take years.

Rodney hastily unlocked and opened the back door of his truck. He jumped on the platform and started tearing the boxes apart like a savage animal ripping through a carcass. The white powder seeped through the packages like flour. By the time Rodney got through ripping up the packages there was coke all over the place. It covered his clothes, as well as on the floor and ceiling of the truck. The smell of the coke's intoxicating aroma filled the truck. Rodney didn't know if the betrayal by Kelli or the coke was messing with his mind. He was feeling various emotions at the same time. He felt like he wanted to kill somebody at the same time as he started busting out laughing realizing how fucked up his shit was. One thing for sure, covered with white powder, Rodney realized he had to take a shower before he could go to see Kelli.

$$\$$$

As they drove off, Carolyn stuck her hand on Abram's crotch aggressively rubbing his instrument. "How fast you think he'll get to Kelli?"

"Quicker than I can bend you over in this car."

"You think she'll bring us to the big dawg?"

"She did the last time. A leopard can't change her spots. She is going down, and she is going to bring a lot of people with her. I can't wait until the great attorney is sharing a residence in Angola with her clients.

S.W. Smith

CHAPTER TWENTY ONE

KELLI

"Damn Rodney, why you come busting into my office like that?" Rodney pushed so hard on the door to my office it looked as if it was about to fly off the hinges as it slammed against the wall.

I turned to my secretary who was right behind Rodney and who looked like she was about to have a heart attack between the confrontation with Black and now this shit.

"It is okay Silvia. This is a good friend of mine."

Rodney had sweat dripping from his brows. He

slammed his fist hard on my desk. I hoped he didn't find out about the packages. I needed to try to diffuse this situation now.

"Baby, what a pleasant surprise."

"I've been told you're nothing but a two bit drug dealer."

I turned away from him because I still wasn't sure how I was going to handle this.

"So, it's true, all the money, the office, the house, the cars, that's drug money."

"Look, I wanted to tell you before. I was getting out of it especially since I met you. It happened when I was married to my husband. I could never make that kinda of money practicing law."

"And you used me to make deliveries. The feds are on to your whole operation."

"Look, I needed to keep things going until my practice picked up to get out of the business. The money for the tennis shoe factory, where do you think that came from? You used me! You never questioned how I could get a bank officer to give you a loan without you having any collateral. You know as well as I know, banks don't loan money to people who need it, only people who already have it."

"They want me to cut a deal to turn you in."

"You can't break up our family!"

"What family?"

"I wanted to tell you before, I'm pregnant."

"Pregnant? What do you mean pregnant?" The anger dissipated from Rodney's eyes.

"I just found out about this. I didn't expect this news when I went to the doctor this morning." The tears began to flow down my face.

Rodney walked toward me and put his arms around my shoulders.

"We are going to work this out. Me and you, babe. You know I would never turn you in."

"Just like I figured, sucker," I thought to myself.

"Baby, I gotta finish some legal work. Can we talk tonight?

"Sure, just don't work too hard. I need my angel to get all the rest she can."

"Sure, sweetie." I gave him a big wet smack on the lips and walked him out of my office.

I couldn't wait to get back into my office. I pulled open my desk drawer and pulled out a jewelry box, the top compartment covered with earrings, but the bottom compartment was full of coke. I put a fist full on my desk and began to inhale with my straw.

Damn, sometimes inhaling this shit was better than an orgasm. I had begun using the stuff at least three times a day. It was the only way I could bring myself into the office. And, of course, I needed it to get through the day. And then again I needed it to have sex all night with Rodney or whomever I was with and make my orgasms stronger.

Shit, I'd better take two hits today because I've got to face Coal and I knew he was not going to be happy.

CHAPTER TWENTY TWO

COAL

Coal's office was located in the Algiers section of the city or "across the river" as the locals called it. From downtown New Orleans, Kelli took the Mississippi River Bridge to get there. Kelli was still high as she drove across the bridge and since it was dark, seeing the city's skyline lit from the top of the bridge made her eyes widen like a Cajun surrounded by broiled crawfish. Kelli didn't like the situation she was in. She didn't have enough money to pay Black or to pay back Coal what she had owed him for the supply. Now this mess with Rodney.

The diamond tennis bracelet was too bad for her to turn down and it only cost $75,000.00. Plus she had begun to use a lot of the product that Coal had supplied her instead.

Coal's office was decorated in a ghetto fabulous manner. The office was located in a rundown single shotgun style house. Nothing gave the appearance of wealth until you got off the porch into the front room. The front door was made of reinforced steel but had wood on the top of it to make it look like a normal door. All the windows had burglar bars. Inside the screen door sat one of Coal's 350lb bodyguards who resembled the rapper Fat Joe but he was Black. They even called him "Black Joe." He was sitting behind a desk with an AK47. In the room was a 52- inch screen TV set with one side of the screen a split screen, one side showing a basketball game and the other side showing pictures of the perimeter of the house. The entire room was decorated with gold-framed pictures of naked women or pictures of half dressed rappers like Little Kim or Eve. There were no posters on the walls, just framed pictures or paintings.

To the side of the desk were three gold leather sofas with accompanying oak tables. There were gold coat racks, gold umbrella stands, gold vases and a big gold chandelier in the middle of the room. There were five gold pinball machines positioned against the gold painted wall. Like a businessman Coal also had a gold-framed twenty-dollar bill, the first one he made in his business. Two heavily armed beefy men were sitting on the sofas watching the game as well.

Kelli apprehensively rang the bell. She looked up to the hidden camera and smiled. She knew over the years, Coal had gotten ruthless, and she did not like bringing him bad news. Bad enough she didn't have all the money to pay him, but she knew she was going to have to tell him about the situation with Rodney. Coal was not going to be happy. An intercom system buzzed her in.

She faked a smile. "What's up gentlemen? Coal wanted me to come down and chat with him."

Black Joe spoke up. "Well, you know I couldn't even let your cute ass in here without Coal requesting your presence, Counselor. I still gotta search you."

Damn that Coal is a paranoid mutherfucka. I have been knowing his butt for fifteen years and he still has someone search me everytime I come into this mug, Kelli thought. At least he got this big fine good looking body-guard this time. I don't mind so much him putting his hands on me this time. The last one, though, was so ugly, his mama probably wanted to send him back after birth.

"Sure, not a problem."

Kelli was still a little high from her hit, so she was horny at the bodyguard's touch. He was kinda cute for a big man.

"Go right in, Coal is expecting you."

Kelli went into the third room from the front where Coal was behind a desk counting a stack of Benjamins , he had just pulled out of a laundry bag. In this room was a plasma 64-inch screen TV that was flat against the wall. His Glock gun laid flat on the desk within arm's reach. If this place wasn't in the middle of the ghetto, it could be featured on Cribs, too. Coal looked aggravated and he had a mean look on his face.

Kelli went over to kiss Coal on the cheek, but the gesture did not change his expression.

"Coal, man, you don't look too happy to see a sistah."

"That depends, if you got my money, I'm happy, if not I ain't"

"Come on Coal, I've been knowing you all these years, you got to give me a little slack here, distribution on my end has slowed down a lot."

"Yea, and what would make distribution slow down?"

"The feds approached Rodney with a deal."

"You know I told you not to get that square involved in the first place. Rodney has never been in the game."

"I know, but it worked for a while."

"I am going to eliminate this problem for you, but now I need $50,000 on top of the money you owe me for expenses."

"Damn Coal, we've been knowing Rodney since grammar school. There is no need to eliminate this problem."

Coal yelled, "I ain't going to the cage for nobody. You should know that shit. I ain't letting the choir boy cause me time."

Kelli slipped. "Damn, Coal you would kill your own brother if necessary."

After this remark, Coal's eyes became piercing daggers that cut Kelli's eyes.

Kelli sought to change the subject. "There is no need to eliminate this problem. I talked to Rodney. He is solid. Rodney would take the time rather than see me go to jail."

"Yea, what makes you think that?"

"I told him I was pregnant."

"Are you?"

"Yeah." He doesn't need to know the truth either she thought.

"And how does that translate into me staying outta the mess?"

"Coal, the only way the feds can get to you is through me, and I would do whatever time or die before

131

I sell you out." Although the words came out of Kelli's mouth she knew damn well she would never do a day of time or die for Coal. She just hoped he believed that shit.

Coal's demeanor turned stern again. "Whatever Kelli, I've got a lot of shit on my mind right now. Make sure you have my money before the end of the week or you will become a problem. Later, Kelli."

Kelli left the office scared. She knew that Coal was no joke. And yeah, he would kill his own brother if necessary. Although no one told her, she always knew that's how her husband, Coal's brother, died. He was about to rat out Coal

$$

"Man bring your fat ass in here," Coal yelled.
"What's up chief?"
"I need you and Angel to take care of someone."
"Too bad we can't let Sheena in on this shit."
"Fuck Sheena. That bitch got dick whipped and

did something stupid. I hope she rots in jail."

"No problem, boss, just give me the name, and we'll handle it."

CHAPTER TWENTY-THREE

RODNEY

Rodney was walking down the sidewalk when Angel and Black Joe appeared behind him. Rodney continued to look for an address to deliver a package that he was holding. Angel and Black Joe walked quickly behind him. Rodney, sensing something wrong, looked behind himself to see Angel pull out a gun. Rodney ran behind a car and Angel took a shot at him. Rodney was breathing heavily. He sprinted quickly down the street. Angel and Black Joe were close behind. Rodney looked down at his shoes and smiled. Angel took another shot at him and the bullet whistled pass his head. Suddenly, Rodney took off running twice as fast as he once was. Rodney got to a seven-foot wooden fence in front of a house. His hands grabbed the top of the fence and he ran on the wood before he easily leaped clearing the top of the fence. Angel and Black Joe looked at each other in amazement lowering their guns. Rodney landed safely on the grass on the other side and ran away from the fence. He looked down at his shoes and smiled "Bullet Sneakers, faster than a speeding bullet."

Rodney continued his route back to his truck. Angel and Black Joe got into their Black Hummer and drove to Rodney's house, parking the vehicle a short distance from his door.

Out of the house came Rodney's mother, Ms. Freda. Angel looked at Black Joe, and they both got out of the car. They walked on opposite sides and grabbed each of Ms. Freda's arms. Ms. Freda looked up in shock and turned her head to each side. She yelled, but became silent when Angel showed her his gun. They placed her into the Hummer, Angel in the back, Black Joe driving.

Rodney was back at work telling the crew about the two guys who tried to shoot him. One of Rodney's co-workers picked up the telephone and shouted Rodney's name.

"Grab the phone, man."

Rodney interrupted his conversation with the other fellows and picked up the phone.

"You got away mutherfucka, but we have your mother. Get your ass over to the warehouse on St Claude and Almonaster now. And you better not bring anyone or even think about calling the man."

Rodney was silent and stared straight ahead. He slammed down the telephone and yelled "I got to go." Rodney ran out of the door and jumped into his IPS truck. He turned on the ignition and sped off toward the warehouse.

Rodney thought, all these years I tried to do the right thing. I never bought a gun even though I coulda had a number of them cheap off the street. Damn, I never thought I would be in a position to need one and not have it. All these years at IPS, all I wanted to do was open up my own business and make some money. I shoulda did the same thing the people I grew up with; played the game. I probably would have been a millionaire right now if I had hustled like everybody else. I wouldn't have had to struggle and they damn sho wouldn't be messing with Moms right now.

Rodney stopped his truck about two blocks from the warehouse. From the back of the truck, he pulled out an extra long iron jack used to fix flat tires on a truck. He ran toward the warehouse and slowed down when it was within sight to sneak around the back. Rodney peeked into the window and saw Angel and Black Joe sitting in front of his mother who was in a locked cage. The cage was large enough for her to stand in, and she could fit her hands through the bars. Her arms were handcuffed. A rag was in her mouth, preventing her from talking, but the chains on her hands were long, so she was able to move her arms somewhat. The warehouse was full of abandoned boxes that looked as if they hadn't been touched for years. There were a number of stairwells leading to the loft. The only occupants this place had probably seen in years were the rats that were frequent to this part of town since it was so near the industrial canal. There were rat droppings over everything—the floor, the boxes and the stairwells.

"Now, Ms. Freda, I let your arms stay free because you kinda remind me of my mama, but if you take that rag out of your mouth, I am gonna have to tie you up," Angel said.

Black Joe just shook his head. "Man, my momma used to beat the shit out of me with an extension cord, before her skank ass just abandoned me. If she reminded me of my momma, I would have put a bullet in her ass already."

Angel laughed. "Man, it could have been worse. What if she would have sat on you? If she was half the size of your fat ass, that would have really caused you some damage."

"Oh, you think that's funny?, Let me tell you about your mama. Man your mama is so fat, instead of a polo on her shirt, she can carry the whole horse."

"Yeah, I got one for you. Your mama is so fat and round, I could paint her yellow and stamp Goodyear on her ass." They both laughed.

Rodney noticed a door on the back side of the warehouse that was not visible to Angel or Black Joe because of a wall that blocked their view. The handle on the door was not locked and gave easily in Rodney's hand. He snuck in the back door and immediately hit the floor with his jack. He quietly dragged himself toward his mother, collecting the rat droppings on his clothes and hands as if they were lint.

"Man, you got me laughing so hard I got to pee." Angel announced to Black Joe. He walked outside the front of the warehouse, leaving Ms. Freda alone with Black Joe, his back to Rodney.

Rodney immediately jumped up and smashed the jack on Black Joe's head, busting his skull, causing brain and blood to ooze from it. He fell hard on the ground and crashed his head onto the side of the cage. Ms. Freda was covered with Black Joe's blood.

Angel, hearing the noise, ran back into the warehouse. He saw Black Joe on the ground and was startled by all the blood scattered around the cage.

"What did you do?" Angel yelled.

Rodney ran toward the back of the warehouse behind the stairwell.

Angel took a shot at Rodney. The bullet was deflected by the stairs.

Before Angel was able to run behind Rodney, his neck was caught by the rag that had been in Ms. Freda's mouth. Ms. Freda tied the rag around the bar of the cage and looped the other end around Angel's neck. She used all her strength to pull both ends and lifted him, and pulled his neck close to the cage. With all the kicking and struggling Angel lost his balance and fell on the cage causing it to turn over.

Before Rodney could respond, he heard the crash of the cage hitting the ground on its other side and the breaking of Angel's neck. The cage's fall backward almost caused his neck to sever from the rest of his body. Angel lay lifeless on the top of the cage, which was now on top of Ms. Freda.

Rodney got to the cage and tossed Angel to the side. "Ma, are you okay?"

Ms. Freda, spread out on her back, pointed at Black Joe's body. "He has the keys."

Rodney checked Black Joe's bloody pants. He

found the key and opened the cage allowing his mother to come out.

He helped her to her feet and gave her a big bear hug, but he was unable to hide the tears in his eyes.

After a moment, Rodney took the card of the FBI agent out of his pocket and handed it to his mother.

"Ma, call these people. Tell them what happened. I got to go."

"Wait, where are you going?"

"I have to talk to Kelli."

"Son, she is involved in all this, I know it. I heard them talking. The big fella was called Black Joe and the other one Angel. They didn't care if I heard them talk. They were going to kill me and you and cut up our bodies with that chainsaw over there. They all worked for Coal. She holds the drugs for him. She distributes the poison. Is that the same Coal you used to run with in school? I thought y'all were friends?"

Rodney was silent. It was the same Coal. We were a crew back in the day. All those years of friendship thrown away for money.

"I know Ma, but I still need to talk to her. When the FBI comes tell them where I am."

S.W. Smith

CHAPTER TWENTY-FOUR

COAL

Since Angel and Black Joe were off taking care of Rodney and Sheena was in jail, Coal really didn't have anyone to take care of problems that needed to be eliminated. Coal had a number of women he dealt with that he set up in apartments in their names and paid all their expenses. Coal would keep safes in each apartment that contained money and drugs. Coal knew these women were afraid of him and if the apartments were ever raided by the police because the apartments were not in his name, they couldn't build a case against him. Also all the women had chidlren and he told them from day one if

143

they ever turned against him, he would not only kill them, but their family as well. This situtation worked well for a long time for Coal. That was until one of the women, Lanessa, hooked up with a Haitian boyfriend, Beaud, who was a small time hustler with ambitions of getting bigger. Beaud convinced Lanessa to stage a robbery with Coal's money and drugs. He told her he would always protect her and she didn't have to worry about Coal.

He came by her apartment with one of his boys, Philippe in his 1965 red Cutlass and took the safe from the apartment while Lanessa was home. They rifled the place and broke the window trying to make it look like a burglary. Lanessa left and went to the Palace Club where she knew Coal would be. She made sure he saw her. She pretended to be drunk and danced all over the place, even cuddling with Coal at one point in his chair. When she returned to her apartment that evening she immediately called Coal on his cell. She sounded hysterical.

"Coal, baby, we have been hit. The apartment has been broken into, and their is shit all over the place"

"I will be right there," Coal assured her.

The first thing Coal did when he got to the apartment was to go straight to the location of the safe. When he saw it was not there, he exploded.

"Who in the fuck would have the audacity to rob me?" He stared an evil glare at Lanessa.

"You sure you don't know nothing about this?"

Coal, baby, you think I'm stupid; I would never steal from you."

"You better not have."

Coal stayed the remainder of the night at the apartment with Lanessa. He was fully strapped with an Ak-47 and a Barretta. Lanessa was more scared than she had ever been in her life. She didn't sleep the entire time, worried that Coal would figure out she was involved and kill her. The next day Coal told her he was going to take a look around the complex and see if anybody had seen anything. He told her that she had to come with him.

Coal's first stop was to the manager's office. He told them that his apartment had been burglarized and asked him had he seen anyone hanging around.

"I didn't see anyone hanging around, but I did see a red Cutlass parked outside around 6pm that night."

Coal turned to Lanessa. "Don't your Haitian friend have a red Cutlass?" Coal had seen the dude around and knew he was Lanessa's friend.

Lanessa couldn't deny it. "Yeah, I didn't know he was around here yesterday. He lives in Algiers, I can take you to his house." Lanessa was trying to think how to get out of this mess. She liked Beaud, but not enough to die for him. She knew that if Coal found out she was

145

involved, he would kill her and her family. It took about thirty minutes to get to Algiers. Coal drove his car and Lanessa sat in the passenger seat, quiet, the entire time. Coal knew if Beaud had his stuff, Lanessa was involved, and she would get the same punishment.

Beaud lived on the second floor of the Fisher projects. Coal and Lanessa took the stairs up the grimy stairwell. When they reached the apartment, Lanessa knocked hard on the door. Coal stepped back into the stairwell, so he couldn't be seen through the peep hole. When Beaud saw Lanessa, he opened the door without hesitation. Coal stepped in behind her, Baretta in hand. Beaud had no gun.

Lanessa said, "Coal thinks you took his stuff, and he wants it back if you did."

She was trying to hint to Beaud that Coal didn't know for sure. Phillipe came into the room with his gun and hand concealed in his pocket.

Beaud pleaded. "I don't know what you talking about. I didn't steal anything from you man."

"I know you got my stuff and I want it back now."

Phillipe yelled. "I don't know why you coming in here with all this bull shit man."

"Chill, Phillipe, man why don't you just come in and let's talk this over?"

"I ain't got shit to talk about, I just want my stuff."

146

"Man, why you let him come in here and disrepect us like this?"

Coal saw Phillip's hand stir in his pocket. Since Beaud was barely dressed and he could see both of his hands, he knew he wasn't strapped. Phillipe was another story. His eyes were glued to Phillipe. When he saw Phillipe's gun come out of his pocket, he raised his and shot him straight in the chest.

Lanessa let out a scream and ran toward the back of the apartment. Beaud dived to the floor. Coal shot Lanessa in the back before she could reach the doorway. Had he been thinking, he would have shot Beaud before Lanessa because Beaud had a chance to grab Phillipe's piece and shoot Coal. When Coal saw the gun in Beaud's hand he had enough time to dive to the floor. The two shots Beaud was able to let off hit Coal in the leg. Before Beaud could shoot again, Coal shot Beaud in the head.

Coal's wound was bleeding profusely. He knew he had to get out of there before the police came. As his blood dripped to the floor, Coal limped out of the apartment into his car. He could hear the sirens in the background as he drove away from the scene.

When the police got to the apartment, they checked the pulse of Beaud and Phillipe and realized immediately they both were dead. Lanessa had lost a lot of blood, but she still had a pulse. By the time the EMT arrived, she had gained consciousness and the police asked her who had done this. The only word that she could utter was "Coal," but the police knew exactly who she was referring to.

Coal was in so much pain and had lost so much blood he decided to go straight to Baptist Hospital. He collasped in the emergency room and was taken immediately into surgery. The surgery lasted eight hours and the doctors were unable to save his leg. When he awoke from the anesthesia, he knew immediately that his leg was amputated. Instead of a doctor's bedside manner to comfort him, he saw two policemen hovered over him. They read him his Miranda rights and arrested him for two counts of murder and one count of attempted murder. Coal knew better than to ask who lived; instead he remained silent and closed his eyes, trying to figure out how he was gonna survive a long stretch of time without his leg.

CHAPTER TWENTY FIVE

SHEENA

The lawyer told me if I pleaded guilty to second degree murder, then the judge would treat it like a manslaughter and only sentence me to ten years. Because it was my first offense, I would get credit for time served and three for one good time, that is, I would get credited three days for every one day I served. In reality I would be out in three years. She told me since I faced life in prison this was a good deal. I had completely trusted the way she handled the situation up to that point so I figured it was probably the way to go.

I got more depressed when she told me that Coal

was arrested on a double murder and that he was facing the death penalty. When I asked her about the details, all she said was he had killed some Haitians in Algiers, across the river. I knew if I hadn't been in here, I would have been able to take care of the Haitians for him.

That was some messed up shit. I loved Coal like a brother, and if I hadn't fucked up he wouldn't be in the jam he was in. I could have taken care of those dudes myself, and it wouldn't have been a problem.

I decided to take the deal after she told me that. With Coal off the street, I wouldn't have a job to go back to anyway; my family was gone. The night before I was set to plead, I couldn't sleep at all. I kept thinking about all the people I had aced and the ways I had killed them. Funny, for the first time in my life, I knew I was wrong for killing even though everyone of those muthers probably deserved it. The little sleep I did get, I dreamed about the murders in graphic detail. The entire night, my life passed before me and I hadn't even died.

I pleaded guilty before the Honorable Judge Melvin Dewey the next morning. He canvassed me about my intent to plead guilty. He asked me had anyone promised me anything in exchange for my guilty plea or coerced me or forced me in any way to plead guilty. I knew what my lawyer said about the time I would get, but I didn't say anything about it because she said it wouldn't be cool to say anything about it at the time of the plea and the judge had already committed to it. I just said no to all the judge's questions and told the judge I was ready for sentencing.

It was too late when I realized that I had fallen for the trap, and Blondie had gotten over like a fat rat. The judge accepted the plea and sentenced me to fifty years without benefit of parole or suspension of sentence. I couldn't breathe when I heard fifty years. I turned to my lawyer, and she smiled at me and said, "Chico said 'hi.'"

So that was the deal that bitch was working on. I was so pissed that I bitch-slapped her skinny butt to the floor. The blow to her face was so hard, there was blood on my hands. The sheriff deputies surrounded me quickly, and I started swinging at them, too. I took out a few of them before a night-stick to my head took me down. I was led back to the jail in a semi comatose state. I couldn't believe what the fuck just happened. Even though I was floating in and out of consciousness, I knew that I had just gotten a fifty—year sentence with no chance of getting out early. I could appeal the shit, but what chance would I have? It was my word against the lawyer's, and I had said before the plea that nothing was promised to me. No way I could do 50 years of anybody's time. That was the same as life.

CHAPTER TWENTY-SIX

KELLI

I was trying to get a hit on before lunch when my office door swung open. I still had the powder on my nose. I knew I should have locked the door, but it was only going to be a quick hit.

This time Rodney showed up unannounced, covered with blood. I wondered what happened to him. I was surprised Silvia didn't come running in here with a scene. She must have been to lunch with her dramatic self.

"I know what happened. You sent those guys to kill me."

"What are you talking about? I wouldn't do anything to harm you."

Shit, I knew I couldn't trust Coal for one minute. Coal must have tried to fuck him up.

"Your associates in your drug dealing scheme. You thought I was going to turn on y'all so you told them to kill me. That powder is really clouding your thinking."

"That's absurd. You know I love you." I tried to sound as sincere as I could as I slowly opened my desk drawer for the small caliber revolver I had just bought yesterday. Between Black and Coal, I figured I had better have some protection around, but I guessed I was gonna have to use it sooner than I thought. With the blood all over him, I would claim self-defense. What the hell, I was a lawyer I would figure out something for killing him.

"You love me, yeah, right. The only love in this room was the love I had for you. I wanted to make you my wife."

Rodney reached in his pocket and tossed out a ring box on the desk.

"You used me to make deliveries for you so I became a drug dealer, too. But I figured by marrying you I couldn't be forced to testify against you. I would have done the time for you."

I opened the box and in it was a diamond ring. It

was only a half of a carat. However, the idea of Rodney still wanting to marry me and doing the time moved me so much that real tears started flowing down my face.

"I never intended to open up that factory with drug money. I would have opened it on my own one day. So here is the money back I got from the bank."

Rodney laid a check on the desk.

"Where do we go from here?" I hesitated when I asked the question.

"You got the only other woman I ever loved involved in this. My mother almost died today and she wasn't part of the deal. Call me a momma's boy, but I love my mama too much to have her go through this again. I love you Kelli, but I am telling the Feds everything about you, about Coal and about the deliveries.

I reached into the drawer quickly and pulled out the gun. I tried to regain my composure, but the tears would not stop flowing. I finally realized I did love Rodney, but it was too late. I had to kill him so I wouldn't go to jail. I pointed the gun at a surprised Rodney.

"How about I shoot you and the tale dies with you?"

"I guess you never loved me."

"I love you, but I have a twelve year old to think about. I have it made, and I am not going back to the ghetto. I've seen what jail does for you, and I am not dealing with that either."

I held the gun higher, pointing at his eyes. The sight of his eyes, still loving though I was about to shoot him caused me to hesitate. I lowered the gun to point at his chest."

"I can't do this."

I didn't know that the FBI was surrounding the building as I was running my mouth with Rodney. I should have just shot him. All of the sudden, they busted down my door. Silvia, of course, had told them where to find me.

Agent Walker saw my gun and just started shooting. Damn, she was fast, no hesitation. I didn't even see her draw her gun.

I didn't feel the bullet pierce my chest. I guessed it even got close to my heart because I felt like I had the worst case of heart burn I had ever had. I knew I wasn't going to make it when I fell straight back and hit the floor. Damn, I got blood all over my Gucci suit.

I heard Rodney yell, "Stop" and felt him next to my body. He was just a fool in love.

I could barely keep my eyes open, but I did see the agents in my office lower their guns.

Rodney was hugging me now and when he pulled me away to look at me I could still see the love in his eyes.

I had to get these last words out.

"I need you to do something for me."

"Look baby, anything you need." Rodney was sobbing.

"I need you to take care of Tisha. We never had anyone once her father went to jail. All my family is gone. She has no one. Raise her as if she was yours. "

"I can't raise a girl. I ain't never been a father. I can't..."

"You can, your heart is good. She needs someone with a good heart."

After I said that it seemed like my body just froze up. I couldn't say or feel another thing. I must be dead. Damn, I wish I had gotten out of the game when I saw Rodney again.

TWENTY SEVEN

SHEENA

Once my appeal was denied, I requested that I be put back in the general population. What the fuck? It is no way I could have survived being by myself for fifty years. I had a lot of enemies around here. I rather take my chances with them than with the solitude. What would be more painful, death that came by one of those motherfuckas or from my own tortuous dreams. Both scenarios were unappealing, so I chose to go and get it over with quicker. I was a bully with no friends here. I

had no alliances and no protection. I started fights with
all the leaders because I wanted them to come at me hard.
I wish someone would take me out of my misery. I knew
it was a matter of time before they would strike. I used
to be creative when I killed people. I wondered when I
got iced would it be original or just plain dull.

I saw all those girls staring at me and talking
behind my back. This was some messed up shit.

I didn't give a shit about no mutherfucka in here
though. I wished someone would bring it on It had been
a long time since I fucked someone up, and I knew it was
time. Sometimes that shit was better than sex. Bring it
on!

CHAPTER TWENTY-EIGHT

SHEENA

Damn, this 250-pound bitch jammed the lock on the door with a bed sheet and hit me from behind. She must have used some kind of stick. I fell to the floor and she kicked me in the neck. She kept kicking me in the neck until it was hard for me to breathe. I tried to get up, but she started stomping on my chest. It was getting harder and harder to breathe. I could see the sheriff's deputies trying to get in, but she jammed the lock real good with those sheets. She was jumping on me like a trampoline, and I kept going in and out of consciousness. Damn, that shit hurt. I felt like blood was coming out of my eyes and mouth. At least when I killed somebody, it was quick and painless. I didn't realize how cold it would be when my time came. Will those guards ever get that gate open?

CHAPTER TWENTY-NINE

TWO YEARS LATER.

RODNEY

Rodney and Tisha were outside playing basketball in the playground. They were smiling and enjoying the hot weather. Rodney dunked the basketball. He was wearing bright white Bullet sneakers, and his emblem stood out large as he hung from the hoops.

"Now top that!"

Tisha grabbed the ball and bounced it high; she caught it in the air and shot a jump shot before she landed. They both started laughing at her feat.

A city bus passed the playground with a sign that

had a picture of Master P holding a Bullet sneaker. The sign read: Bullet Sneakers: Run Faster, Jump Higher.

Tisha pointed at the bus.

"I can do anything with my Bullet sneakers."

Ms. Freda ran past them after the bus.

"I am going to work."

Rodney shouted after her. "Ma, I told you for the last two years, you don't have to work. We have made it."

She continued to run. "I know that. I want to work."

Even though the bus continued on its way, Ms. Freda ran and caught it.

Rodney and Tisha watched as Ms. Freda sped past the bus and waited at the bus stop.

"Look at her go!"

"Yeah, Bullet Sneakers."

LOOK FOR S.W.SMITH'S NEW BOOK

HITTIN IT

They loved Sex, Money, and Bling Bling. Meet Lanesa, Patrice, and Wanda: three sisters from New Orleans. They wanted it all, and they would go to any means necessary to get it.

Patrice's friend and neighbor took her man, her money, and her home. Now, she's out for revenge and the world better watch out. Her motto is "revenge is a dish best served cold."

Wanda, a lawyer for only a year, lost her license and the life she had always dreamed of when she was set up by her employer.

Lanesa worked at the airport checking in luggage for departing flights. When passengers left town, she knew exactly where to go to rob them and meet all her financial needs until that one day when she robbed the wrong person.

Forsaking regular 9 to 5 jobs, they decided the only way to get rich was to use their wits as well as their bodies. But when one of them turned up dead, the fun and games ended and the other two had to decide if they wanted to continue the game or get out before it was too late.

AVAILABLE NOVEMBER 2004

ON SALE NOW

THE

CONNECTION

MURDER,
MONEY,
SEX,
AND A
WAREHOUSE FULL OF COCAINE

BY S.W. SMITH

Chapter One

Nina never wanted to be a lawyer. It just seemed like an extension of a good hustle.

She always considered herself a smart heifer. In high school she graduated third in her class at Booker T. Washington, the local public school in New Orleans. She went to class, listened to what the teachers had to say, went to her grandmother's house where she stayed, did a little homework, and waited until Granny fell asleep so that the party could begin. School just came easy to her. She could stay out all night, go to school the next day, and make an A on a test with no effort whatsoever.

Nina's mother was a prostitute, and she couldn't tell you who in the hell her father was. Her mother became a dope fiend and she did ten years on a violation of probation, possession, and crack sales. Granted, she was only selling the shit to support her habit, but the prosecutors couldn't care less and instead of rehabilitation, she got straight up jail time. It was her third offense. When she got out she was so happy she didn't even bother going home; she went straight to her pimp and scored some heroin. She overdosed and died the same day of her release.

Nina figured that her problem was she was too much like her mother.

"I like dick and I like to party. I would have sucked and fucked for free, but too many motherfuckers were willing to pay for the shit, so I gladly obliged," she bragged to her friends.

Nina was raised by her grandmother in the Magnolia Housing Project. Her grandmother was so nice and had gone through so much shit with her mother, Nina always wanted to make sure she never knew what went on after she fell asleep. Nina would sneak out at night through the back screen door, and it would be on. She charged about a hundred dollars for the pleasure of her company. She would do whatever and take it wherever they wanted to put it. She would save the money or buy a nice outfit to party in. Nina would only wear the outfits at night to party at the bars. Business was always good. She was a good looking chocolate brown sister with green eyes, light brown hair and a big ass.

"The green eyes I probably got from my father 'cuz my mother sure didn't have them," Nina told anyone who asked about them.

She used to fantasize about her father a lot. She figured he was probably white which would account for her hair and eyes. She would imagine he was probably smart, maybe a Tulane Professor or something like that because she could read books and quote entire passages from them, after one reading. After all, her test scores were always in the top five percent of the city and she was always getting academic awards for something. She didn't give a shit about any of that, but it made her grandma happy, so she did the little bit she had to do to keep the accolades coming.

What she did care about though was that older men wanted her bad. She would usually pick the most influential looking man in the bar. She would check with the bartender who claimed he ran with her mother back in the day and he would tell her the deal on the fresh fish. All she needed to know was what kinda job the Negro had and if he could pay. She would act all sexy when she first met them and they would think she was twice her age. They would get a hotel room, and she would not let them know she was in high school until the deed was done. She would usually want to get out of there quickly especially if the mug couldn't lay the pipe right so she would just accidentally drop her School ID card out of her purse and say out loud, "I loved being with you, baby, but classes start real early in the morning, and if I am not on time they give out detentions." At that point, the men would usually ask how old she was. She would innocently tell them fourteen, the age that would have classified their sex as statutory rape in Louisiana. They would be so scared, she would get her fee and a big ass tip to boot, just to keep quiet. The entire ride home they would be begging her not to tell anyone because they didn't want to go to jail. Before she snuck back into the house, she would buy a dime bag of hydro with the proceeds and get seriously high until she fell asleep.

When she wasn't getting down she was just chillin' with her girls, Wanda and LaTisha.

I guess you could say Wanda and LaTisha were her posse. They didn't like getting down as much as she did, but they had their own little hustle, namely shoplifting. Wanda and LaTisha would go to work in the mall like a pair of tag team wrestlers. They had various methods of stealing and these ladies were good. There were so many ways of detaching merchandise from department stores that they never used the same scam twice.

Once Wanda pretended she was blind and needed so much attention from the store clerks and security guard she kept bumping into that LaTisha easily made off with about $2,000 worth of stuff without blinking an eye.

In another store, Wanda in open view placed numerous objects into a shopping bag as if she was going to steal them. She also placed a number of objects in her bra like she planned on stealing them. The store security closely followed Wanda as she walked straight to the front door past the cashier. Before she made the step out of the door, she quickly turned back around to the cashier and dumped everything in front of her register, even the items in her bra while pulling out a roll of bills to pay for them. While all of this was going on, Latisha easily shoplifted about $4,000 worth of goods.

They got along well, especially since Nina supplied the dope and the location of the parties. She partied hard with her girls. She figured she owed it to herself after a long week of hustling.

Her senior year she met Carl and he was so good to her and good at doing her, she had to stop the con and games. Carl was a good looking, tight-six-pack having, weightlifting, basketball playing, lovemaking fool.

When she first saw him, Nina lit up like a candle. She

was hot for him quickly. Carl was a freshman at Dillard University. He lived on campus and was a serious student. They met at a party on campus and although he was with his boys and she was with her girls, they immediately made a connection and hooked up. She was dancing on the floor with some light weight, hip hopping to Scarface when she saw his eyeballs staring her down. She continued to dance, but stared right back at him as her partner tried to keep up with her moves. Right after the dance, he walked up to her as the DJ was changing the song, put his arm around her shoulder, and said to her dance partner, "Yo, Shorty, my baby sister and I need to talk for a minute, I hope you don't mind." Since Carl was 6'6 and a solid 260 pounds all the brother could say in return was "Yea, dude, no problem," and walked away.

Nina, on the other hand, said, "You don't know me like that."

"You are right, I don't know you like that, but I want to get to know you like that, and that kid on the dance floor was blocking the gate. Let's dance, and let me get to know you like that."

They danced every song together until midnight.

Yea, she did sleep with him the first night. He took her back to the dorm room and laid her ass out. She got aggressive with him first while she was sitting on his bed watching TV. She began gently rubbing his chest and circling the nipples on his chest with her fingers. He had a six inch gold medallion with the initials C and F hanging from his neck which she used to gently scrape at the light black hair under his chest. She could see the rise in his pants as she got rougher with his chest. She slipped her hand down to his belt and started unbuckling his pants and pulling down his zipper. As she cupped the outside of his bulging boxers with one hand, she brought her tongue down on his right nipple and she flicked it up and down with her tongue. Then she covered his nipple with her entire mouth and began sucking it like it was a piece of barbeque rib bone. He was getting off on that; she could feel his underwear getting wet with her other hand. She slowed her pace. She moved onto his left nipple with her mouth, and used her other hand on his right nipple to keep it warm while she sucked his nipple hard. After a few minutes of this, he was moving around under her and put his hand on her butt. She knew he was ready to get busy now, so she took her tongue and guided it down his chest. She stopped at his navel button to eat that for a little bit then slowly made her way to his big fat dick. By this time it had busted out of his boxers and was standing straight up.

She couldn't wait to get that juicy thing in her mouth. She told him to take off all of his clothes. She left the room and went to the common area and came back with a chocolate candy bar she had gotten out of the vending machine. She unwrapped it and put it in the microwave for ten seconds to melt. When she got back to his dorm room, he was lying stripped naked on his back, penis still standing straight up. The only thing he had on was his medallion. She spread the chocolate on top of his dick and licked it off like she hadn't eaten for days. At first she gave it a hard thrust in her mouth, then she started moving her mouth up and down on his penis gradually picking up speed like an Accera passenger train. Her hands were still on his nipples, and she was squeezing them hard. She pulled her mouth off his dick because she could taste that he was about to come. Talk about sweet and sour sauce-the juices from his penis and the sweet taste of chocolate. Carl was moaning the whole time.

She stopped and started flicking the shaft of his penis to calm him down. She had all her clothes off by that time and she just jumped on him, placing her vagina on his penis. Every time he moaned she squeezed the lips of her vagina tighter and pushed her pelvis closer to his thighs.

His eyes were closed, and by the smile on his face she could tell he was really enjoying this shit. He turned her over on her back and just started pushing his dick harder and harder into her. She was wrong when she thought he was about to come. He kept this up for at least a half hour.

"I am about to come. Do you want me to come now?"

Carl's voice was shaking.

She didn't reply, she just contracted her vaginal muscles to squeeze harder on him. He grabbed her butt with his hand and just started pumping harder into her. She couldn't move, she just laid there and let him thrust up and down into her.

When they came, there was pussy all over the walls. Fluids exploded onto the sheets. They got even deeper after that since Carl told her about his life up until he met her.

He was from New Haven, Connecticut and his father and mother were Muslims. He grew up in the mosque and believed it was important to keep your body a temple: clean from drugs and alcohol. He wasn't a practicing Muslim at that point in his life, but he maintained a lot of their principles.

"My father and mother were killed in a car accident five years ago on Christmas eve. The cops were chasing someone they thought committed a robbery when the man drove his pickup onto the exit ramp east on the I-91 North expressway. He drove his truck into my parents' car. I was still in high school and had to move in with my aunt. She hired a lawyer who sued the cops since the man who had hit my parents had not committed the robbery but had just sped away from the cops because he was on parole. I got a little change, but the judge in the case said it could only be used after I got out of school. That was cool with me because I always liked school anyway. When I moved down here the only thing I kept besides my clothes was this chain my parents gave me for my birthday before they died."

He held the gold medallion tight with a sad look in his eyes. Nina tried to lighten up the situation.

"I thought Muslims weren't supposed to have pre-marital sex," she teased him.

He looked her straight in the eyes and said, "Only with a woman we intend to marry."

Nina was shocked; she didn't know if he was playing or not, but he looked so intently into her eyes that she figured he wasn't.

He changed her life. After he came into it, she lived, breathed, and died for that man. Since he was serious about his books, she became serious about her books. Carl wanted to be a lawyer. He thought she would make a good one too. His dream was for both of them to go to law school and after law school open a law practice together.

After class they were always together. Carl didn't smoke, drink, or get high which meant Nina no longer smoked, drank, or got high. He also didn't eat meat, that was dead meat, so for all practical purposes Nina became a vegetarian.

Her girls couldn't believe the change in her. They

thought that she wouldn't keep it up for long and sooner or later she would be back to her old ways. Didn't happen. Nina loved Carl and wanted to make him proud, so she stayed straight.

They still partied. They went to bars, discos, college dances, and any social event you could think of. And they hung out with friends who drank and smoked, only they didn't. After she graduated from Booker T. Washington, she went straight to Dillard University. She went to school year round, and was able to graduate in three years in the top of her class with honors, like Carl. They then focused on the LSAT. Nina scored a 759 and Carl scored a 780 out of a possible 800.

He wanted to stay in New Orleans, so Tulane University Law School was their first choice. Their grades and test scores made acceptance a sure thing. Being in law school made them even closer. They got an apartment together, and life revolved around school and each other. Tulane had given them both full scholarships, and student loans paid for anything else they needed that wasn't covered by the scholarships.

Something about law school made Carl even more horny because they were always at it. Most of the other students at Tulane were snooty and rich. You could tell that their people had money and Nina thought they looked down on them as lucky niggers who really could never be in their league. She just ignored them. Carl could always out debate everyone, and because of her photographic memory, Nina only had to read the cases one time and she could recite them word for word for the professors.

Although law school was tough, a love of a good man helped Nina to sail through. Her favorite subject was criminal law. She would analyze the cases and argue with the professors for hours about how the defense of a criminal should have been conducted. Carl always told her she would handle the criminal defense work in their firm. They were looking forward to graduating in a few months.

They always went back to her grandma's apartment in the projects on Sundays and enjoyed a big meal with her. She was a great cook. She always would fix barbeque chicken, beef ribs, two types of greens, potato salad, candied yams, coconut and chocolate cakes, and sweet potato pie.

One night they were coming home from Nina's grandmother's house after Sunday's dinner. Instead of driving from her house, they usually walked, although it took them through some of the worst parts of town. Nina didn't mind. It was a good way to work off some of that big dinner and her big fine man was there to protect her. Carl always told her she should never be afraid of her own people.

They were joking about the people in their class when

two dudes with ski masks approached them from behind. The men both had guns and stuck them in their backs, yelling at Carl and Nina to hand over the money. Nina had a feeling Carl wasn't going to let this go down like that. She just handed over her purse and said, "There is about $250 dollars in the purse. Will you take it and just leave us alone please?"

The robbers took the purse and told Carl to hand over his wallet and jewelry. Carl gave up the wallet with no objection. When one of the robbers went to snatch the chain, Carl's hand instinctively grabbed his arm. The other robber yelled, "Yo bro, you gonna let him punk you out like that."

A 38-caliber pistol rose from the robber's other hand. The sound of the gun froze Nina in time. Carl fell backward and the chain snapped off of his neck into the hand of the shooter.

"Next time don't go trying to punk a real man," the robber yelled as Carl fell backwards. "Yo bro, let's go."

Carl's head hit the pavement hard. The blood squirted all over the street. Nina bent down and held him tight. She tried to scream loudly, but no sounds came out of her mouth. She felt for the cell phone in Carl's pocket and dialed 911.

"My man has been shot! I am at the corner of Claiborne and Washington Avenue, please send help!"

Carl never gained consciousness. He lay there bleeding until the ambulance arrived. She held him the entire time praying that the life from her body would be transferred into his. But nothing happened. Because it was so obvious that he was dead, the ambulance attendant would not even allow her to accompany him to the hospital. She rode in the back of a police car. The policemen who responded to the murder needed a statement, and despite the fact she was covered with blood and had lost her only true love, her soul mate, she was transported to the police station.

She couldn't help them one bit. Her mind went dark. Too dark to talk. The pain she felt was so intense. Every time she attempted to open her mouth to speak, tears just rolled down her face. She was unable to tell them anything about the man who murdered Carl. That night her love became just another unsolved murder.

The police department's psychologist thought that she suffered from post traumatic stress syndrome since she could not say what happened but thought that later on something might happen to trigger her memory. Her grandmother and cousin Trevor picked her up from the police station and brought her home. She stayed there in her room for two weeks. She vomited every one of those days, although the only food she consumed was a few spoons of soup that was gently forced down her throat by her grandmother.

Carl's aunt had his body brought back to New Haven where he was buried. Nina was so upset she couldn't even attend the funeral in New Haven or the memorial service they held in New Orleans. The newspapers and TV news programs had extensive coverage on the murder. The fact that Carl was a promising law student and that his murder remained unsolved played for big headlines.

Her cousin Trevor stayed at the apartment with her grandmother and her. He was somewhat obese but strong as a bull. Trevor would do all the handy work around the house but never had much to say. After two weeks in her room, he and her grandmother thought if she didn't come out of her state, they would end up burying her.

Trevor came into her room, picked her up, and brought her to the bathroom where her grandmother was waiting to clean her up. He gently set her down on the toilet seat where her grandmother washed her face with a warm washcloth and proceeded to clean the rest of her musky body. As she dressed her she began to speak, "Carl would not have wanted you to mourn him like this.

He would have wanted you to go on with life and to finish law school."

Nina didn't answer her. She knew she had no intention of returning to law school.

"Trevor and I are taking you to the doctor's office. You have been vomiting too much, we both are worried about you."

Nina didn't remember Trevor carrying her to the car. Nina didn't remember actually riding to the doctor's office. Nina didn't even remember being examined by the doctor. But the one thing she did remember about that day was the doctor telling her she was about three months pregnant. She began to cry savagely. Her man had left her another beginning.

ON SALE NOW

BUY IT TODAY!!!

About the Author

S.W. Smith grew up in the ghettos of New Orleans, a few blocks from the Magnolia Housing Projects. After graduation from law school, Smith set up a law practice in the middle of the ghetto, the same area of town where Smith grew up in. Before quiting the practice of law, S.W. Smith has become a successful criminal defense attorney who represented numerous clients accused of murder, armed robbery and the sale of drugs.

To schedule author's appearances: call (203) 772-1344 or email swilk10@cs.com

Solmar Publishing Company, LLC

ORDER FORM

The Connection
Murder, Money, Sex, and
a Warehouse Full of Cocaine_____ $13.00

Dawg Tales_____ $12.00

Shipping/Handling (per book)
(Via U.S. Priority Mail)_____ $4.00

Quantity_____

TOTAL_____ $_____

PURCHASER INFORMATION

Name:_____

Address:_____

_____

City:_____State:_____

Zip Code:_____

BOOK CLUBS DISCOUNTS!

Please mail Check or Money Order to:
Solmar Publishing Company, LLC
129 Church Street, Suite 420
New Haven, CT 06510

To order by phone, Call (203) 772-1344
Toll free (888) GLORY-90
Online ordering: swsmithbooks.com
or email swilk10@cs.com

Solmar Publishing Company, LLC

ORDER FORM

The Connection
Murder, Money, Sex, and
a Warehouse Full of Cocaine_____ $13.00

Dawg Tales_____ $12.00

Shipping/Handling (per book)
(Via U.S. Priority Mail)_____ $4.00

Quantity _____

TOTAL_____ $_____

PURCHASER INFORMATION

Name:_____

Address:_____

_____

City:_____State:_____

Zip Code:_____

BOOK CLUBS DISCOUNTS!

Please mail Check or Money Order to:
Solmar Publishing Company, LLC
129 Church Street, Suite 420
New Haven, CT 06510

To order by phone, Call (203) 772-1344
Toll free (888) GLORY-90
Online ordering: swsmithbooks.com
or email swilk10@cs.com